MERELY
A MISTER

Other Books by Sherry Lynn Ferguson

The Honorable Marksley
Lord Sidley's Last Season
Major Lord David
Quiet Meg

MERELY
A MISTER

•

Sherry Lynn Ferguson

AVALON BOOKS
NEW YORK

Library of Congress Cataloging-in-Publication Data

Ferguson, Sherry Lynn.
    Merely a mister / Sherry Lynn Ferguson.
        p. cm.
    ISBN 978-0-8034-7461-1 (hardcover : acid-free paper)
    1. Aristocracy (Social class)—England—Fiction.   I. Title.
PS3606.E727M47 2012
813'.6—dc23

                                                    2011033935

PRINTED IN THE UNITED STATES OF AMERICA
ON ACID-FREE PAPER
BY RR DONNELLEY, HARRISONBURG, VIRGINIA

For my eldest, who knows that noblesse oblige

Chapter One

Myles woke coughing. The room was dark, though sunlight edged the windows' heavy drapes. At bedside Phipps, his valet, hovered, holding a candle and a draft.

Myles weakly shook his head. Waving Phipps to the far side of the room, he concentrated on regaining his breath. As he struggled, he eyed the flustered manservant. Phipps could not be bettered when it came to dressing. The man had an exquisite hand with a collar. But he knew little of the sickroom. *Why should he?* In four years' employ with Myles Trent, Lord Hayden, the valet had never had occasion to test the necessary skills.

Myles closed his eyes, stifling another cough. Despite his precautions, he verged on a decline—another period of inexplicable illness. The night's troubled dream served as warning, presaging the coughing, the fevers and the infuriating indisposition.

Infuriating, because Myles worked at making himself strong. He had always walked, run, raced, ridden, swum. He boxed regularly and often, until he was the last one standing. He had been disciplined in diet and drink, discreet with all else. Fortune had favored him with health, intelligence, and prospects. But the doctors had told him long ago, after the incident at the weir, that he had damaged his lungs—that he would forever retain a proclivity for recurrent infection. In all this time he had, perhaps, merely been lucky to have suffered as infrequently as he had. He had been sixteen at the weir; next month, he would be twice that age. He found it curious, how one's body seemed to remember every trifling slight, every abuse . . .

1

As his breathing deepened and steadied, Myles thrust himself upright and signaled Phipps closer.

"Shall I send for a physician, my lord?" Phipps asked.

Again Myles shook his head. "I shall be returning home—urgently, Phipps."

"To England, my lord?"

"Have I another home?" Instantly he regretted his temper. Phipps was invariably literal. "We shall meet the yacht at Bordeaux. And then—perhaps, London—or Braughton—" He could not settle on a destination. He knew only that he could not stay in Italy until the spring, as planned. "We must leave at once." *We must leave,* he thought, *before I am laid low for weeks.*

"Yes, my lord." Phipps frowned. "But Lord Knowles—?"

"Mustn't be alarmed." Myles reached for the mug Phipps had brought in to him. "I shall speak with him at breakfast." He sipped the warm liquid, coughing again at the first swallow. "Zounds! What *is* this?"

"Warm ale and egg, my lord. My granny's truest—"

"'Tis sufficient to be coughing, Phipps. I've no wish to be nauseated. Open the drapes. And fetch me some port."

Myles looked out the open French doors to the veranda, which was bounded by an artfully carved stone railing and a glorious effusion of potted red geraniums. Beyond the railing, Lake Como glistened in the midday sun. Though October had advanced a week, no hint of gold tinged the opposite shore's wooded rise. Myles had been dreaming once more of a lake, but he knew he did not dream of Como, nor of any other Continental lake. He dreamed of home, and of summers as a child. He suspected that the lake he envisaged was in Cumberland.

His friend Knowles would be disappointed by this change in plans, but he would choose to continue on alone. Knowles, and Lord Demarest, and George Glidden, and almost every other young heir to the British peerage had always considered a Grand Tour a birthright. Every one of Myles' circle had craved a return to Europe to see the sites their fathers had visited so freely and with such pleasure. Yet the contest with Bonaparte had long denied them their own explorations. Apart from a tenuous peace a dozen years before, after Amiens—when the armies of Europe had temporarily stalled, and Myles, among a few others, had slipped briefly over to France—the Continent had proved a battle-ground. Some frustrated youngsters had bought regimental colors and chosen to fight rather than stay away. Tragically, many of them had never returned. Tens of thousands had lost their lives just that summer at Waterloo.

His brother, David, had nearly been among them.

Again Myles closed his eyes. David had been fortunate; the family had been fortunate. Myles could not recall any of his acquaintance who had escaped mourning over the past twenty years. Even Chas, his cousin, had lost parents and a grandfather. And all suffered now for the losses at Waterloo in June. Myles would forever remember the shocking lists of casualties, the makeshift hospitals in Brussels, the blasted, burning countryside. Monsieur Bonaparte, he thought grimly, had much for which to atone. He considered the Corsican's isolation on St. Helena a fit-ting penance for so acquisitive a warrior.

Myles shed the blankets and swung his legs to the side of the bed. He wore only his small clothes to bed. Given his preference for sleeping with a window open, and the chilly morning breeze from the lake, he reached for the dressing gown Phipps had placed across the covers. Despite his fatigue, Myles knew he must arrange as much as he could over the next day, before his energy failed him. He must see to transportation, the servants, Knowles . . .

He stepped through the open veranda doors and looked out upon the sparkling water. Cousin Chas, who had designed the gardens for another villa along this very shore, had long extolled the joys of Como: the alpine air, the extravagantly charming vil-las, each with its unique character and display of flowers and stately evergreens. The cypresses outside Myles' suite marched along the drive at lakeside, mimicking the magnificent mountains that hemmed the view. The place was truly spectacular. All the more curious, then, that Myles should have discovered such a desire to leave it.

He had been wandering contentedly enough for some months, ever since parting from David and Billie in Brussels. He and Knowles had toured Cologne, Munich, Vienna, Trieste, Venice,

Milan—and now paused at Lake Como. They had intended to stay for some weeks before traveling on to Florence, Rome, Naples, and perhaps the Aegean. Whether Lord Knowles would adhere to the same plan now was questionable. In Milan, Knowles had succumbed to the charms of one of that city's renowned sopranos; indeed, Myles, who had known his friend Knowles since starting school, had only ever seen him silenced by two things: a challenging game of whist and now, the lovely voice of Signorina D'ellesandra.

Whether the affair with the signorina was a serious matter or not, Myles did not presume to guess. But he believed his friend should be let to find out. The task at breakfast, then, would be to convince Knowles to continue in Italy. Myles, knowing he was fading, could not impose upon his friend to accompany him on such a hurried journey home.

When Phipps returned with both coffee and port, Myles sipped at both before washing. Then, choosing rest over the rigors of dressing, he took a seat out on the veranda and settled his heavy brocade dressing gown about him. He remembered this weariness from previous declines—the headache and lack of appetite, the unconquerable lethargy. Now, though, he considered his age. He had not felt so very old when he had set out upon this ramble, but he was reminded again of his impending birthday. Staring at Como's waters, he again recalled the struggle to free David from the depth of the weir. He had known then, for a certainty, that had he not surfaced with his brother he might as well have drowned with him. Yet what could he claim to have accomplished in all the years since?

At a knock upon the door, Phipps admitted Knowles.

"I must say, Hayden, that I am rarely so much in advance of you. In your smalls yet, I gather, and the hour close upon one! Why, you'll scarce be through breakfast before we're due at Sandy's party! Not that *he* would notice what time any of us arrives. Nor what we're wearin', for that matter. Probably think your dressing gown all the crack! Though I did promise to host a table at cards for him tonight—"

"My friend, I shan't be attending Sandringham's soiree."

Knowles showed his surprise.

"Why ever not? Thought you liked Sandy, even if he is a bit green. And you must admit that the old earl had fine taste in property. This is a lovely little spot, to be sure, but Sandy's villa in Bellaggio there, across the water—"

"You should go along if you wish, Knowles. But I must prepare to return home."

"*Home?* Confound it, Hayden, whatever can you mean? We've that much more of Italy to see. We are to stay here at least 'til November—"

"And so you shall. The Villa alla Solle is yours for as long as you wish it. You might find you even desire to invite your *bella* D'ellesandra—and her mama, of course—to share it."

"Bella! But her name's Natala—Ah!" Knowles' ears reddened as he caught Hayden's gaze. "I s'pose you think me a fool."

"No, my friend." Hayden smiled. "I think you susceptible."

Knowles laughed. "Yes, I s'pose. But heaven help you, Hayden." He shook his head. "It shall be something worth seeing."

"You are most unlikely to see me similarly enamored, Knowles. When I return home, I intend to marry."

"*You?*" Knowles abruptly took a seat. "Who?"

"I've no idea. Perhaps Avis Birdwistle. I'm told she has been trawlin' for me long enough. Fact is, I shall be thirty-two next month. The thing must be done."

"Look here," Knowles said, examining his face too closely. "Are you certain you feel quite to rights? You look a bit peaked this morning."

"No more so than the usual. I confess I could use more sleep." He forced another smile. Knowles could not suspect him ill, else Hayden would never be rid of him. Whatever his more immediate inclinations, loyal Lord Knowles would insist on seeing his feeble friend home.

"I have another year on you, Hayden, and no younger brother, either. You don't see me rushin' off to the altar—"

"Perhaps you should consider it."

Again Knowles' ears reddened.

"She does sing beautifully, doesn't she? Strikes me quite silent every time I hear her."

"Certainly a rare enough effect."

Knowles took no offense. "You cannot be serious, Hayden. Why such pressing concern now for preservin' the line? There are Trents enough. In a pinch you'd have no objection to David—and given that he's wed Miss Billie—"

Hayden waved a dismissive hand. "'Tis the legacy, my good fellow. Had your father lived, believe me, he'd have been after you as well. Mine is inflexible."

"You've heard from him?"

"Not recently, no. But I feel his cool breath down my neck. 'Tis all so fatiguin'."

Knowles peered at him. "There have been ladies enough—eligible, eager young ladies—in Vienna, Venice, Verona—in every place we've stopped! Why, at Sandy's tonight, I'd wager there will be more than a dozen eligibles! Now that Bonaparte's bested, half the *ton* is touring the Continent. You needn't head *home* to find a bride—"

"The thing must be done properly. I shall consult with Grand-mère and the Pater."

"Surely you've had enough consultation with both of them? I recall you've more often resented it. Your grandmother wishes you only to care about the girl, which I must say doesn't sound at all likely. And His Grace knows you would never select an unacceptable *parti!* Do stay, Hayden. No need for haste. Think of all we've planned! You've talked of it so, all these years—"

"George, I have decided." At the abrupt tone, one that Hayden rarely employed, Knowles frowned. For a moment, at least, he fell silent.

"Well, then," he said at last, "will you let me know where you go? I remember—what was it? Ten years ago? When you hared off abruptly to Yorkshire—"

"Wales."

"Same difference, surely?" Knowles smiled. "Demarest and I heard nothing from you for two months. Then there was the cruise you took on your yacht—I think it was just after Corunna—when you claimed an overwhelming wish to visit Ireland—but tucked yourself into some burrow on the Isle of Wight! If you weren't such an amusin' fellow, Hayden, we'd have dropped you long before this! Send a line, at least, every few weeks, so that I needn't tell tales to those who inquire. I don't care to deceive my friends. And—devil it!—they *do* inquire!"

"I shall let you know where I am. But now, Lord Knowles, I must start on some plans. I must ensure relays of fresh horses. With luck I shall make it across the pass, and through France, and catch the yacht at Bordeaux before any weather threatens. I shall take only a few men with me—Phipps and Perkins, certainly, and probably John and Thomas." Hayden quickly named the two footmen he judged the strongest. "Everyone else might stay on. I've no wish to deprive you of the pleasures of this holiday, Knowles. You must continue to luxuriate. At my expense, of course."

"'Tis most generous of you, though not at all necessary. I confess, this can never be half as jolly a tour without your company. Still, I might stop again in Milan on my way to Rome."

"You do that, Knowles, and then you must send me *your* news. For I've no doubt there would be news."

"I say, Hayden, you're much too forward."

"No more than you should aspire to be. Some other swain might steal her from you."

Knowles' eyes flashed.

"Demme if they will! Well, I mean—deuce take it, Hayden. I shouldn't let you scamper off! I told David I would look after you."

"Did you indeed? M'brother takes too much upon himself. And burdens you."

"You did enough for him! And what of your plans to stop in Paris to see him and his missus?"

"I shall see him—and Miss Billie—earlier than anticipated. At the New Year. They are certain to stop at Braughton before departing for India, if that is what he has decided upon." Hayden gestured languidly. "Now do permit me, my friend, to set matters in motion this morning. 'Tis not as though I intend to slip out while your back is turned."

"Close, Hayden. Very close indeed! I'll leave you, then. But I shall stop back before heading on to Sandy's—" And still objecting, Knowles left the room.

Hayden sighed. He wondered if he even had the energy to

make the arrangements that needed to be made. But yes, he would manage it. If the past were any measure of his stamina, he had as much as ten days or two weeks before the fevers downed him. By then, he should have found a quiet place to recover. And Knowles' mention of Cumberland reminded him that he had always intended to return. Perhaps that lake, in his dreams, was in fact a familiar one, one of the Lakeland waters. He had appreciated the county as a youngster, yet he had not visited even once in almost two decades. Idly, he also recalled that his father had desired him to look into that matter of a letter, something of complaints at one of the northern properties. As he penned the necessary messages arranging his travel, Hayden calculated how many days sailing from Bordeaux might place him up at Morecombe Bay and the Lake District.

In a tortuous nine days, changing horses every twelve miles or so and taking on local coachmen as Perkins needed relief from duty, Hayden's small band fleetly crossed France to the Atlantic. Hayden scarcely noticed the countryside. The roads were abysmal; his coach, though well sprung, jolted and bounced. Though he could occasionally read, more often than not, and despite the discomfort, he suspected he dozed.

Hollow-eyed French country folk watched their passage. Hayden's limited entourage attracted attention because of its haste rather than its grandeur; he heard several muttered references to the demanding "English *aristo*." But the citizens were defeated and weary rather than hostile. Hayden swept on to the coast.

At Bordeaux, the party boarded his waiting yacht. Hayden then gauged his own strength and directed the crew to sail straight up the coast, across the mouth of the Channel and on into the Irish Sea. His judgment in this was faulty, because by the time storms hit them across from Holyhead, he had succumbed to the first of his anticipated fevers. But the sea was still smoother than the roads, and his group pushed on. At Morecombe Bay they coursed through Rennie's excellent canal to the market town of Ulverston, where a most solicitous innkeeper and his wife delighted in hosting m'lord and his small retinue. Funds flowed freely to make his lordship as comfortable as the humble surroundings permitted, though by that time Hayden lay too sunk in fever to commend the effort.

They stayed several days in Ulverston, until Hayden's temperature fell. He then sent a protesting Perkins and the footmen ahead to the Priory, the Braughton property on Ullswater, to check the household and prepare for his imminent residence. By sending the others on, he had hoped to gain a rare period of solitude. Indeed, Hayden felt so far recovered early the next morning that he left his bed and strolled alone about the quiet town. The autumn air invigorated him; he dared hope that this time he need not surrender a month or more to illness.

In the main square off Market Street, a short, stout fellow— the only man about—busily loaded a wagon. The countryman tipped his hat to Hayden, who asked him where he meant to travel on a Sunday.

"I be off to Glenridding, sir. I comes in once a month to sell my vegetables and fleece. 'Tis a better price than in Penrith."

"These are hard times for farmers, are they not, Mr.—?"

"Dilly, sir. I be Lewis Dilly. And you've the right of it, sir, as to the times. Never seen such as this, and like to get worse, so's I hear."

Hayden watched Dilly heave another bundle to the back of his wagon. The notion, when it struck him, seemed both sensible and appealing.

"Mr. Dilly, should you mind a passenger—a paying passenger— on your journey north? I've a mind to go on there with you today, rather than lingering here in town. My own people will take a day or more to send back for me."

Dilly eyed Hayden's impeccable clothing.

"'Tis an open wagon, sir. Not that I'd accept any pay for taking you up, but you're like to find the journey more than you might manage."

"Nonsense. 'Tis a fine morning, without a breath of wind or a single cloud in sight. Your team looks rested and eager. Indeed, I should welcome a turn at the reins."

"Weather's like to change all of a sudden in these parts, sir. Particular this time of year. Could rain by noon."

"I shall take my chances. I've an urge to complete my travels today. Won't you permit me to accompany you, Mr. Dilly? I need only a moment to collect a small bag at the inn. Perhaps they might pack us some refreshments as well."

The offer of nourishment seemed to decide Dilly. Though still dubious, he agreed to wait a quarter hour. Returning quickly to the inn, Hayden had the innkeeper gather treats for the journey, while Phipps packed some necessities into a satchel. The valet complained at being left to await the carriage, but Hayden had no wish to encumber Mr. Dilly with baggage and another passenger. The unusual nature of his decision did not trouble him in the slightest; he was used to answering only to himself. He would arrive at Ullswater tonight, before his people could turn about. And he was eager to settle as quickly as possible, for he acknowledged that his uncertain health did not inspire confidence. But his temperature had been low for much of a day—a record of sorts, given his past experience—so he had every expectation that this time his malady was on the wane.

The wagon proved sturdy and its team frisky. Dilly took them at a fair pace across the flats away from town, talking all the while about the market for wool. Hayden only half heard him, all too aware that as the morning sunlight struck his face, he warmed uncomfortably. He loosened his coat, with some struggle, as it was tailored so closely to his form. At once he felt the autumn breeze. When they turned off the road that led on to Kendal and Windermere, Hayden questioned their route.

"I don't take my team along the sharp turnings on Carmel Fell, sir," Dilly told him. "Not unless I've need to go on into Kendal. This is a much easier path, as you'll see—from the foot of Windermere up through Hawkshead and beyond—and quicker, too, despite the narrow track."

"I told my man I should be going up by Windermere, that is all. It makes no difference."

"I'd not think so. Not unless you be touring, sir, and wish the views from Carmel! But I knew at once you was a serious gentleman on serious business, an' not along for a holiday."

Hayden smiled as he looked away from the driver. Those in

his set would no doubt agree with Dilly and describe the Marquis of Hayden, heir to His Grace the Duke of Braughton, as a "serious gentleman." But as for "serious business," he had no clue what that might be.

"What brings you to the lakes then, sir?" Dilly asked.

"I've come to check on some estates up at Ullswater."

"Estates! Well now, you've that look about you. Managing properties for someone, then, are ye, sir? And who would—"

"Mr. Dilly, do lend me the ribbons here," Hayden suggested indifferently. The moment Dilly knew him for what he was, all ease of conversation would end. "You might do with some relief. I assure you, I am a most experienced driver."

Dilly obligingly, and rather surprisingly, surrendered the reins. The picnic basket on the bench between them had drawn his attention. The team managed little more than a steady walk as they took the incline up from the Greenodd and Haverthwaite flats, but they were not straining. Hayden meant to spare them.

"You've a fine hand, sir. You keep a carriage?"

"I do," Hayden said, adding silently, *several*. But as he drove, he realized that for too many months he had allowed too many others to drive him about; indeed, for too long he had let his father and the obligations of rank steer him, however obliquely. Hayden had long anticipated the Peace and the freedom it would permit, but—despite his curtailed Continental tour—he had yet to feel it. He had always treasured his options, few as he believed them to be. Perhaps, as Knowles suggested, this marriage matter must be delayed yet again. *A man,* he thought wryly, *must make such decisions for himself.*

That brief, ironic thought of rebellion amused him.

At the top of their ascent, having passed the wagon route up from the Windermere ferry, they halted and looked out over the distant heights—the top of massive Scafell and the Langdale Pikes before them, and Coniston Old Man peaking off to the west. The view was grand, boundless, and shifting in color and light, much as Hayden had pictured it in his dreams. Flocks of sheep roamed the green or rested beneath solitary trees. Drystone walls traced pastures and half-cut hay fields before climbing

bravely, sinuously, onto the sloping heights. Each forward movement of the wagon appeared to alter the subtle hues about them,
exposing different prospects.

Oblivious to the glories of his own country, Dilly sat happily
munching the bread and cheese packed from the inn.

"You look a bit flushed, sir." Dilly's brow furrowed. "I'd best
take the team for a spell."

Though Hayden had at first credited his aching head to the
fresh air, he knew the affliction foretold worse. And, wearing
his coat or without it, he was uncomfortable. He wished only to
bear up for the rest of the wagon journey, even if Dilly must toss
him bodily into the load in back.

"I have been ill, Mr. Dilly. And thought I had regained strength.
But clearly, that is not entirely true. Forgive me for proving less
than engaging company."

Dilly protested that he was everything amiable, lent him a thin,
coarse blanket to supplement his coat, and proceeded to entertain himself—by relaying tales only a bored farmer might trouble to follow. Hayden, with no appetite for food or conversation,
slid into the fatigued state that heralded yet another bout of fever.
He chafed at his inability to steal even one day simply to haul his
carcass from one spot to another. But he had come so far, and
was now so close . . .

They passed a small settlement; Dilly told him they were not
far from Hawkshead. Hayden had lost all sense of direction. He
viewed his surroundings through bleary eyes, eyes that could no
longer appreciate a view. Attempting to rally only confirmed his
inability to do so. He clung to Dilly's wagon, and to conscious-
ness, as though everything in life depended upon enduring the
journey.

As the sun blazed, Hayden shivered. He had scarcely attended
a word his companion had said during the previous hour. But
Mr. Dilly must have determined upon another course, for Hayden
was soon aware of strange voices, of strong hands propping him
up in the seat, then pulling him abruptly to the ground, where he
staggered and almost fell. He could identify only Dilly's country
tones—admonishing someone, pleading with another. Two different men urged, "White's—White's."

Hayden tried to shake his head.

"Not the club." His mouth, parched, allowed only a scratchy "Put me down—St. James's—"

This drew guffaws. He attempted to straighten, to correct them, but a debilitating nausea doubled him over. A deep voice remarked, "Aye, sir, I think ye'll be stayin' *here* for a bit, not goin' troublin' Prince George!" In the subsequent laughter, another voice, this time a woman's, sharply urged, "Get him to White's at once. No, Mr. Dilly, Jamie will take him on. There's no better place for him."

Again Hayden objected, but the group ignored him. A burly man who smelled strongly of the farm grabbed his arms and tossed him up roughly, like a sack, upon another wagon bench. There Hayden slumped, aching but vertical. He heard only mutterings and horses' hooves—his senses had deserted him.

After eons, blissfully cool sheets welcomed him. Gentle hands, a woman's hands, bathed his forehead. The scent was unusual. Lavender, he decided. When he opened his eyes, his gaze met the indeterminate half-light of dusk. Or was it dawn? A pair of lovely gray eyes observed him.

"Heav . . . en," he croaked, and the angel laughed.

Chapter Two

I fear not, sir," Anne said brightly. "You live, and must suffer here on earth a while longer." Even as she spoke, her patient closed his eyes.

The intense blue of those eyes lingered. Anne had not expected such a gaze, despite his fair complexion. She surveyed the stranger's fine features yet again, then turned to Ned, her father's man.

"He will elude us for some time, Ned, and fall in and out of fever. If he wakes while I am belowstairs, do see if you can catch his name. Mr. Dilly did not know."

"Aye, miss." Ned moved to the side of the bed. He had readied their visitor for bed the previous night, dressing him in the elegant lawn nightshirt from the single satchel. Ned had told Anne how fit the stranger appeared; despite his illness and the lean look of him, he was well muscled. "A gentleman," he remarked now with certainty.

"Yes, a gentleman," Anne agreed. *A most refined gentleman.* She sighed. "And his family will be concerned. We shall send word on to Glenridding as soon as someone can be spared, as soon as Father returns. But we must have a name! Mr. Dilly will describe him, and that might do. He is rather . . . unique"—again she looked to her patient's features—"but we cannot rely upon it."

"They'll be searchin' for *him* too, Miss Anne."

"Yes. Though I believe—I believe I might make him better— were I to have him for a few days . . ."

"You do work wonders, Miss Anne, with your herbs and such."

"We have been fortunate, Ned. I shall claim nothing more."

14

She left him to go to the kitchen, where Cook tolerated Anne's intrusions only for the needs of the ill. A lavender tea compress had helped with the gentleman's cough the previous night, so Anne chose to employ it again. She thought the cough most worrisome. The fever did not seem so very high; it might in fact have spiked only in response to the challenges of travel. But the cough! There was always the fear of consumption, though he had not been spitting blood.

From the kitchen she could see the corner of Esthwaite Water, a small mirror of a lake down below, just beyond the wooded slopes fronting the road to Hawkshead. In the distance, the very top of Coniston Head beckoned. Farther along to the north, in the mist that made distance so deceptive, the Langdale Pikes rose smoothly serene, their hummocks green, gold, and inviting. Inviting now in the sun, but Anne well knew how dangerous the craggy heights and fells could be and how quickly the weather changed upon them. With their shifting colors and cloud shadows, the mountains always drew her.

Anne finished preparing the compress, then took the stairs again to the spare bedroom. The room had seemed the best choice the previous evening, as Ned often slept in the dressing room between it and her father's bedchamber. Their ill guest necessarily needed a man's attentions. Anne considered the room the prettiest in the house; her mother had claimed it until her death eight years before. The view of the hills from the double windows and the welcome light from the south and west had long made the room a favorite for reading. The dining room directly below it had, for some reason, never captured half as much light.

The maids had lit the fires that morning, since the year moved quickly on into autumn. Anne contemplated all the additional work necessary before the first frosts: those herbs and flowers she still planned to harvest, the infusions and vinegars and oil emollients to make, collecting the cuttings and rose hips. Only when she had entered her guest's room and placed the basin with the compress on a side table did her preoccupied gaze rise to meet her patient's steady blue one.

Immediately, she smiled.

"I am Anne Whyte," she told him. "This is my father's house.

We are in the village of Wiswood, some few miles out of Hawkshead, where Mr. Dilly left you yesterday evening. You were in no fit state to travel on with him. He feared to take you over Kirkstone Pass. You have a high fever, sir. With your permission, I shall attempt to treat that and your cough, as the nearest doctors are a day's ride away. There are local apothecaries—" The stranger began to cough. Anne nodded to Ned to raise him so that she might apply the compress to his chest. "—should you desire one." Gently, she positioned the moist, fragrant cloth, whereupon his coughing eased.

He had closed his eyes once his coughing began and now kept them closed even as he shook his head, which Anne interpreted as a disinclination to call in an apothecary. All the better, since Anne believed herself as capable as any apothecary—or more so. But her patients had always sought her out; never had she imposed her methods on anyone. This gentleman might, of course, change his mind at any point. She was not certain how aware he might be, even now.

As the compress eased his breathing, Anne had the maid Molly fetch a pitcher of rose water, then set about applying a cool, scented cloth to the gentleman's burning forehead. That he should be such an attractive man, even when so ill, was disconcerting. Vain, of course—with such looks, he had to be—but few men had as much reason to be vain.

Molly obviously had no qualms about appearing besotted.

"Molly," Anne remarked as she patiently bathed the gentleman's face, "I think you'd best go collect Tim from Father's office. He has his tasks, but I believe he has time enough to help Ned here in the sickroom."

"Oh, but Miss Anne, I'm only too happy to help—"

"I well know it, Molly, but I believe 'tis best to have Ned and Tim see to the gentleman."

"Yes'm."

Once Molly had gone, the gentleman, who clearly had a keen ear—for he had not opened his eyes—struggled to say, "You thought—her—in danger?"

"I thought *you* in danger, sir." She was rewarded with a laugh, which unfortunately lapsed once more into a cough. *Really,* she thought, *I must obtain some information from him.*

With his next gasped words, he apparently wished to oblige her.

"My name," he managed, "Myles—" But he could not continue.

"You mustn't talk further, Mr. Myles." A frown crossed his face as he tried to stop coughing. "We will sort out what we must once you are able. Until then, you must rest." And Anne interpreted the weak movement of his hand as agreement.

Throughout that morning he slept fitfully, but the compresses did seem to contain his cough. Anne managed to pour some tepid tea into him—of crushed willow bark and chamomile—and commended herself when his fever appeared to lessen. She tried two additional decoctions for his fever, and, by late afternoon, was gratified to discover him awake and half sitting up when she entered the room.

She sent Ned to get his own rest and pulled a chair to the side of the bed. Young Tim stood dutifully at attention by the door opposite.

"You are feeling better?" she asked. For some reason, meeting the stranger's shadowed gaze, she strove to sound merely concerned and courteous. In truth she wished to touch him, to grip his hand very hard, as though to lend him some of her own strength.

"Much, thank you. Though . . . 'twould seem"—and Anne could have sworn he teased her—"my fortitude is to be tested. One draft . . . might have served . . . as well as three."

She smiled. "I would determine the most efficacious, which will no doubt prove the tonic you like the least!"

"I might dissemble."

"No, you cannot dissemble." At his raised eyebrows, she explained, "At the moment, sir, you are too weak to dissemble. Or at that, even to protest."

"You experiment, Miss Whyte."

"You have confessed to feeling better."

"Surprisingly, that is indeed the case," he conceded. "But you cannot discount"—he coughed briefly—"the effect of your company." Anne could not prevent her quick blush. Observing her, he added, "Just please, no laudanum."

"I have never given anyone laudanum, sir. Only the home remedies I devise here from my own garden. But why should you object so particularly? You have had it before?"

Mr. Myles shook his head.

"M'brother—injured at Waterloo. Though it has been months, he has had . . . difficulty . . . weanin' himself."

Anne nodded.

"'Tis a powerful relief for pain. Perhaps too powerful." She paused, then asked, "Is your brother's name David? You spoke of him last night."

"Good Lord." His sigh provoked another cough. "Pray do not tell me I . . . have been indiscreet."

"Not at all. You merely mentioned some names—in considerable distress, I might add. David most frequently, but also Chas."

"Yes, David is m'brother. I have been dreamin' . . . of an accident from many years ago. Perhaps because of the cough. I do not know. Chas is my cousin."

"Tell me how your coughing might relate to the accident."

He summoned a smile and again spoke carefully.

"You would not let that go . . . unremarked . . . would you, Miss Whyte? I was told, when ill before, that I might have weakened my lungs . . . in attempting to stay under water. For some considerable period."

"Because of David?" When he merely nodded, Anne asked, "And have you had such fevers before?"

"Several times—the latest, four years ago. I have learned . . . to anticipate their recurrence. And no"—he caught her look—"'tis not the consumption."

"Yet you were traveling—"

"I have been traveling for two weeks, Miss Whyte. I wished . . . to reach the lakes because of reasons . . . that need not trouble you. My people are at Ullswater, between Glenridding and Pooley Bridge. I should . . . send word."

"We shall happily send a message as soon as my father returns. But just now, I cannot spare Ned or Tim. And 'tis two days lost for anyone else in the village. For the moment, sir, I am glad to hear that you have had these bouts before. I did worry that they might indicate something worse."

When he shook his head, she rose to go, but he stopped her.

"I did not intend . . . to drive you away, Miss Whyte. Do stay and speak with me. Your village is Wiswood?"

She was surprised that he had remembered anything of what she had relayed early that morning. Something in his manner indicated that he expected to be obeyed, though this was *her* home and he was in no condition to contest with her. She had Tim help her straighten the blankets upon the bed; then she returned to her seat and launched upon a description of tiny Wiswood, with its view of placid Esthwaite Water and its open vale, the surrounding pretty beech woods, the sheep crofters and few shopkeepers, and the manor where her friend, Vera Sprague, had grown up and lived before marrying the vicar in Hawkshead.

After fifteen minutes, Mr. Myles' eyes were closed. After twenty, she could tell that he had fallen asleep, which was all for the best, as she had been warming enthusiastically to her topic, one that she could not believe truly drew his interest. Yet he had confessed to wishing to travel to Cumberland, even though he knew himself to be ill, a circumstance that Anne found most curious.

She returned to her workroom off the kitchen. The room, a former pantry, contained stores of dried and drying herbs, oils, tonics, and precious powders, as well as the small still with which she made decoctions. She had been learning and practicing with home medicines for many years, after her mother had first suggested the herbalist's arts as a practical and worthy application for her inquisitive daughter. Anne had been twelve. And now, after a dozen years, she would still "experiment"—as Mr. Myles accused her—but she was pleased to think that her reputation for healing was a good one. Mr. Myles was not the first stranger to have been sent to her, though she had to allow he was the most intriguing. Perhaps, she mused, his advent was a form of a test of her skills, lest she grow proud and complacent.

When her father did not return by dinnertime, Anne knew he was delayed another day. She did not worry about him, since he had made such journeys so many times before. He had taken Simmons with him. And everyone knew her father . . .

She frowned as she entered the guest chamber. Ned had just finished placing a fresh compress upon Mr. Myles' chest. The gentleman's gaze settled alertly on her face, though he in all other ways looked his weariness.

"Why the lavender?" he asked simply.

"You do not like it?"

"I do like it."

"That is why." She moved closer, to the side of the bed. "Few people dislike the scent, so it aids in masking the camphor oil and other herbs, which some find less pleasant." She examined his strained features. "Have you a headache?"

When he nodded, she assured him, "I shall get you more tea for it. I came in to ask if you've any appetite for something else. Some broth, perhaps, for dinner?"

"No, nothing at all, thank you. Though I cannot say it is flattering—that *that* should be your reason for coming to see me."

"If you can speak so, sir," she said lightly, "I must believe you healthier than I had supposed."

"I think you must be an angel."

"You suggested that earlier today. You have had a fever."

He laughed weakly.

"You will not permit me to compliment you, Miss Whyte."

"Oh, but I will. Once I know you to be restored to good sense."

"Perhaps there is little of that for restoration."

"Then I fear you need stronger medicine than I might supply." She smiled. "There is apparently nothing the matter with your *mind,* sir, however much your head might pain you. Do let me get you something for it at once." And in considerable relief, she fled to her herb closet, where she leaned a moment against her worktable, too aware that her cheeks were hot. She was flirting with the man, with a stranger in her care. Indeed, her behavior struck her as little better than Molly's.

In some perturbation, she set about heating his willow tea, all the while assuring herself that *he* had been flirting with her as well. *He must be most seriously ill,* she thought, laughing as she gathered the tray.

"Has your father returned?" he asked her as she entered the room. "I would speak with him."

"He has been delayed. I now expect him by tomorrow night."

"He is often away?"

"Within the past few months. He . . . he takes brief journeys."

"Yet you manage here on your own."

"I do." She took a chair at bedside and handed him a cup of the willow bark tea. "I am hardly on my own. But you mustn't talk, sir. You are more fatigued than you allow."

His gaze followed her as she straightened the blankets at his side.

"What of your mother?" he asked abruptly.

"She passed away seven years ago, when I was seventeen." Anne raised her chin.

"You look younger." As she felt herself color, he persisted. "You've no brothers or sisters?"

"I had a sister, two years older than I. Sarah died in childbed three years ago. Her husband has since remarried and has started a family in Newcastle. I have visited, but they are not . . . not truly family."

"And why are you not wed? How is it that you have not accepted an offer?"

Anne glanced briefly at Ned, who sat on the opposite side of the room. She knew her single state was a topic of discussion among the servants. But Ned appeared to be nearly half asleep and not in the least attentive.

"You presume that I have received offers?"

"I do not presume. I assess."

"You *assess* because I do not wear a mobcap. Yet at twenty-four, I am distinctly on the shelf."

His eyebrows rose. "How tediously rustic," he drawled, which immediately set her back up. "In town, you might have anyone you wished."

"In *town,* sir, which you seem to know so intimately, not only my age but my small portion would prove an obstacle. You must know that."

"As the sorceress that you are"—again he coughed—"I imagine you might enchant someone into forgetting any failing."

"I think you should not speak anymore here tonight." She rose from her seat. She now believed she might not like him quite as much as she had suspected. "Clearly you grow confused, to think me both an angel and a sorceress."

"Angel *or* sorceress, they are both the same. Out of the ordinary." As he coughed, she reached to take the teacup from his hand, carefully avoiding touching his fingers.

"I have never before been complimented quite so *elliptically,* sir." She felt his forehead. "Your fever seems to have lessened. Ned will see you ready to sleep again. And he or Tim will call me tonight should you need me. Good night."

He watched her somberly as she collected the tea tray, then closed his eyes without attempting an answering "good night."

Anne spent some time reading in her notes and reference books about coughs and fevers. But as she prepared for her own bed, the subject of her reflections was not her patient's illness but his manner. He struck her as more than usually privileged. Though unfailingly polite, the ease with which he anticipated service surprised her; he had no self-consciousness regarding the requisite, continual attentions of Ned and Tim. His habit, she decided, was to be served. And he appeared to think it quite within his purview to quiz her about the most personal of matters, while relaying very little of himself. True, she had not encouraged him to talk, and, given his illness, she had not wished to pry, but still . . .

The next morning, she braved his room in better spirits, having determined that as her patient, he must exhibit greater compliance, however used to command he might be.

"You look much improved this morning, sir." Indeed, a healthier color highlighted his high cheekbones. The expression about his eyes was still grave. His eyebrows, she noted, were much darker than his distinctively fair hair. But, though his lips hinted at a readiness to be amused, she thought he could not be a particularly cheerful man in the usual way.

"I see you come to do battle this morning, Miss Whyte."

"Why should you think so?"

"Your chin is most determinedly high. Do you think this the lion's den?"

She laughed. "If so, sir, I am well armed. Did you not know that lavender is famously said to tame lions and tigers?"

"I wonder who dared prove it?" And he also laughed, a very pleasant laugh indeed, until it devolved into a cough. Anne and Ned helped him sit up against the pillows and fitted him with another compress.

"I think you should attempt some breakfast this morning, sir. You must maintain your strength, even with a fever. What do you usually take?"

"Port." At her shock, he added, "I rarely eat breakfast. Should I grow fat, I would not fit into my coats."

"I should not have imagined you so much a slave to fashion."

Again his eyebrows rose, but she could not interpret his gaze. She had thought at first that he was pleased, but there was a frown between his brows.

"'Tis clear you have little familiarity with town," he said.

"That is not something I have ever claimed. I have never been to London." Again she raised her chin. "Will you now accuse me again of being 'rustic,' as you did yesterday?"

"I beg your pardon. I intended no accusation. 'Twas most ungracious of me. And as for never visiting London, you are the better for it." He turned his head and gazed steadily at the painting over the bureau. "I shall try whatever breakfast you choose to bring me, Miss Whyte."

"As you are so obliging, I shall bring you something with port." She felt rather than saw him watch her as she left the room.

Anne had Cook make some of her excellent porridge. That, and some warm milk to thin it, accompanied one of the morning's fresh-baked rolls and a small jug of Anne's specially boiled syrup of port, honey, anise, and currants.

When she returned to him, he was sitting up farther in the bed, and one of her father's heavy dressing gowns covered his arms and shoulders.

"I was told your father would not mind," he said, catching her look.

"Not at all. Ned did exactly right." And as she smiled at Ned, the manservant turned bright red. "You must take a break now, Ned, and send Tim up to us. I shall sit with our visitor while he eats."

"Shall you?" her patient asked softly. "I assure you that I will make an effort."

"I do not question it. I simply thought you might prefer some company."

He eyed her with some amusement.

"You are a liar, Miss Whyte."

"I have never had anyone say so."

"They have not caught you at it."

"So now I add 'liar' to 'angel' and 'sorceress'! I fear you are still feverish."

He simply smiled. Having sniffed her syrup, he poured it liberally over his porridge, then manfully sampled the result. " 'Tis very good," he pronounced, "but not sweet enough."

"You have a sweet tooth, then?" She smiled. "Sugar is expensive. I must use honey. But the honey might ease your cough."

"I should have guessed that you are always prescribing." Again his attention shifted to the painting over the bureau. "The Langdale Pikes," he said. "Do you see them from this house?"

"Indeed, yes. From this very room. You know the Lakeland well, then, sir?"

"Reasonably. I spent some summers here as a boy. Now I see to properties north of here, at Keswick and Ullswater."

"You are an estate agent, then? Mr. Dilly implied as much to the men who brought you."

"It is one of my duties," he said, directing his efforts to the porridge.

"But you live in London."

"Usually. I have just returned from the Continent—from Italy."

"Italy!" Anne looked at him in wonder. "Surely that would have been a much more congenial climate for one with your—your malady?"

"Congenial it may be. Nevertheless, I grew ill there."

"And traveled all this way! 'Tis a wonder you are here at all!"

"I might suspect you, Miss Whyte, of preparing the ground for a miracle cure. *'He was doomed,'* " he stressed, another spoonful of porridge hovering in his hand, " *'yet I saved him.'* "

"I have never *saved* anyone."

"Then why am I eating this porridge?"

She had to laugh. "'Twill relieve your symptoms, which is all I have ever claimed to do. Much of the time, that is enough."

"The local apothecaries must rage at you."

Anne shrugged. "As I mentioned, there are not many. Our blacksmith, Booth, is our bonesetter. And there are several mid-wives. One apothecary, Mr. Albright, in Ambleside, is quite elderly. I have learned from him and consider him a friend. The others, as you say, may rage. But I have never taken payment, which must satisfy them."

"Quite the contrary—as your healthy patients deprive *them* of pay." He smiled at her. "How did you start upon this course?"

Anne nodded toward the painting over the bureau. "You've noticed that painting."

"Yes. 'Tis very well done. Did you paint it?"

"No, my mother did. And more than a dozen others hanging throughout this house. She was most talented, a talent I do not share. But she encouraged me from a young age to find an interest. When she lent me my grandmother's herbals, I started to read about herbs and their qualities. I had grandmother's receipts and collected others from everyone I met. Father permitted me to plant anything I wished here in the garden. I have tended to it now for a dozen years. When I go into Kendal, or Lancaster, I purchase the few items I do not grow, like camphor oil and cinnamon. But now that I have my own still, I need purchase even less. You must be aware that we Cumbrians are known for our thrift," she added lightly.

"I have heard that. Though opening one's home to a stranger, feeding him, clothing him, and giving him round-the-clock care would seem to dispute such a claim." He stopped eating as he observed her pink cheeks. "Perhaps you can afford to be so generous because you are thrifty."

"I think you are very used to amusing yourself, sir."

"Quite right. But not at your *expense,* I hope, Miss Whyte. As you are so thrifty, 'twould be most unforgivable of me."

She laughed, which seemed to please him. As he pushed his tray away, she rose to take it from him.

"And now," he said, tapping the compress on his chest, "I should like to rid myself of this—and get up."

"You will not leave bed today, sir. You need another day's rest."

"I am feeling much better," he said, and his blue eyes appeared to darken. "I have not coughed these twenty minutes. And I have been through this before."

"Too many times, apparently," she said equably. "And probably because you have risen before you should. You still have a fever. You must rest." She thought he looked remarkably stubborn and concluded again that he was a man very used to prevailing. She stood straighter.

"Is this the *price,* then, for your generosity, Miss Whyte? That I must be imprisoned in this room?"

"You have just had port for breakfast," she countered quickly.

To her surprise he laughed, a wonderful, relaxed laugh, which she suspected was more than rare. But the laugh again led to a fit of coughing. Anne had Tim hold the gentleman upright while she fumbled in her apron for one of her horehound drops. She pressed the lozenge into the side of his mouth, then gently rubbed his back, a back that was surprisingly broad. As the coughing subsided, she and Tim again propped him against his pillows. He mouthed the horehound drop as he watched her.

"I do not deny that you are much improved, sir," she said, pulling back from him to stand to the side of the bed. "Even your desire to be up, and your evident high spirits, tell me you are better. But you have been placed, by whatever fortune, in my keeping, and so you shall stay until you are well enough to fight me. And at the moment, Mr. Myles, I think I should get the better of you."

His eyes narrowed.

"Do stop calling me 'Mr. Myles,' " he said shortly, the command somewhat impeded by his effort to avoid swallowing the lozenge.

"Is that not your name? Ned said—"

" 'Tis not—'tis not proper. You sound as though you are my nurse."

"But I *am* your 'nurse.' And what about it could possibly be improper? Shall I call you only 'sir'?"

"You needn't call me anything at all," he said, gesturing dismissively. "Though 'sir' would certainly be preferable to 'Mr. Myles.' In point of fact, I am—"

"Oh, miss!" Molly knocked upon the open door as she curtsied. She boldly ogled their patient, only reluctantly turning her gaze to Anne. "Mr. Wenfield's come to call! He's down in the parlor. An' ever so anxious to see you—" The maid's attention drifted once again to their fair-haired guest, who did not acknowledge the girl in the slightest.

"I must leave you, sir," Anne said abruptly, wheeling to the door. She closed it behind her and Molly with marked satisfaction. If a sign of her patient's improved health was this prickly temper, she thought—in some temper herself—that she must keep him sedated.

In the parlor, Perry Wenfield, looking every inch what he was—a young gentleman of considerable means—rested one smartly booted foot upon the raised stone hearth. He was an attractive man with carefully styled amber locks and rather too consciously earnest brown eyes. Anne had met him frequently at assemblies since the spring. His father leased Hollen Hall, a magnificent manor several hours to the north, but Perry had been at school, or traveling, or in town, for much of his family's tenure.

"Miss Whyte!" He came forward eagerly to take her hands. "It is too early to call, I know, but I came around from Kendal this morning, and the small matter I attended to in Hawkshead took no time at all." He beamed at her, but Anne could never quite summon the energy to beam back at him. "It has been several weeks since we met at the Ambleside assembly."

"Yes, I believe it was three weeks ago." He seemed pleased that she remarked on the calendar. She asked him, "How are your parents?"

"Doing splendidly. Very well, indeed. They sent you their regards, should I happen to see you."

Anne thanked him for the communication, relayed her own best wishes to the Wenfields, and asked after his business in Kendal. He had been there to consult a solicitor about a possible purchase of property. His father, it seemed, having made a considerable sum in shipping, hoped at last to build his own house. As fond as they were of Hollen Hall, as beautiful as it was, they felt it time—after eight years—to surrender the lease and move to a home of their own.

"The Duke of Braughton will find another tenant for Hollen," he said, "with a snap of his fingers, I dare say."

"But certainly no tenants as responsible as your parents, Mr. Wenfield," Anne said graciously. "And will you not need a place to live while you build your house?"

"Oh, we shall keep the lease for a good part of the next year. These things always move along at a creaking pace, don't you know. Doubtless the kind of pace old Braughton finds convenient." He winked at her, which Anne found she could not quite like. "The best aspect of this new property—where my father wishes to build, that is—is that it is just over on Windermere, closer to you here at Wiswood." His look suggested his satisfaction, which Anne found most discomfiting, especially after the wink. Though she thought Perry Wenfield pleasant enough company, she would not have wished him to live closer; she would have preferred that the Wenfields and Whytes should have many leagues between them.

"Miss Whyte, I stopped today particularly because—well, at the assembly at Ambleside, we had rather a grand time dancing, did we not?"

Anne agreed politely, though the Ambleside assembly seemed ages ago. The topic bored her. Her thoughts had tripped back along upstairs to ponder her patient.

"I should like to do it again sometime," Perry added.

"What? Oh, of course. Dancing with you is always a pleasure, Mr. Wenfield."

"I believe we get on very well together."

"Indeed, Mr. Wenfield. You are most agreeable company."

He bowed. "I assure you, I feel *very much* the same. And so I hope that you will, that is—that you might give me permission to speak to your father."

"My father is still traveling, sir."

"Yes, I was informed. But on another occasion—and soon." Again he looked most serious. As her father, Everett Whyte, was often consulted by his acquaintances, Anne smiled.

"You do not need my permission to speak to him." She was finding it increasingly difficult to converse with Perry Wenfield. She wished he would depart and leave her to her ministrations upstairs. "If you'll excuse me, Mr. Wenfield, I have a seriously ill patient just now."

"For what I wish to say to him—your father, that is—I should prefer to have your permission—Anne."

The use of her name in that tone, and Perry Wenfield's particularly pointed gaze, had Anne looking at him in dismay. She knew he would be considered an eminently proper suitor. But she did not consider him; she had scarcely given him a thought between meetings at assemblies.

"Mr. Wenfield . . ."

"Perry."

"Mr. Wenfield, you do me a very great honor. But we do not know each other well at all. Such an interview with my father would be premature."

"Would you permit me, then, to call again—and soon—so that we *might* know each other better?"

"You are welcome to call, sir. But you should know that I do not keep regular hours."

"Might I make an appointment then, Miss Anne?" he asked playfully. She sensed he meant to drop down on one knee; she stared at him in some horror. She had never before had an offer from someone so thickheaded.

"I think 'twould be best if we were to remain simply friends for the nonce, Mr. Wenfield. I do not wish to leave my home or my tasks here in Wiswood. To put it very clearly, sir, I would prefer that you did not speak to my father."

He looked disappointed but by no means dissuaded.

"I respect your concerns, of course, my dear Miss Anne, though I've no intention they should hinder *us*." His gaze suggested her wishes must match his own. "I shall make every effort to attend you as often as you permit. My happiness, you see, depends on persuading you differently." She thought his smile, and the confession, too confident.

"I truly must return upstairs, sir."

"If you must." When she kept her hands hidden from his, he bowed once more and quit the room.

Anne sighed and looked to the ceiling. Perry Wenfield! She heard him with his tiger outside; they were returning at once to the north and Hollen Hall. Perry barked his commands much too loudly and disagreeably. There was no necessity for such insupportable noise here in such quiet country. As she mounted the stairs, she caught a view of his curricle, a racing curricle that struck her as impractically jaunty. Somewhat, she thought, like Perry Wenfield himself. But then she remembered that Mr. Myles might wish to send a message to Ullswater, and she quickly opened the window on the stairs.

"Mr. Wenfield," she called down, "might you wait five minutes and carry a letter north with you?" Wenfield tipped his hat to her and, handing the reins to his tiger, jumped down to wait to the side of one high red wheel. Anne waved her thanks to him, then hurried upstairs. She collected her writing box from her room before entering her guest's.

" 'Tis abominably early," he said crossly, "to be making calls and braying in the streets."

"Is there a better time to be 'braying in the streets,' sir?" She saw that he repressed a smile. "Mr. Wenfield waits to convey a message to your people at Ullswater, should you wish to send one. I might write it for you."

"I've no difficulty with my hands, Miss Whyte," he said, offering both to take the writing box from her and to place it on his lap. Quickly he drew paper, quill, and wafer from the neatly arranged interior and opened her small inkwell. Just as quickly, he wrote no more than four lines, before signing and folding the sheet. He sealed the missive with the wafer before writing the direction.

Anne noticed that he wrote with his left hand. His script was bold and clear, but Anne could not read it until he passed it to her.

"Pray thank Mr. Wenthorpe for me."

"Wenfield," she corrected absently, already on her way out of the room. As she passed downstairs she read the direction: *Mr. Phipps, c/o Mundy, The Pier House, Pooley Bridge,* which told her nothing at all.

"Who is this mysterious patient of yours?" Perry quizzed her. "A sweet biddy who has discovered a fondness for your teas?"

Anne did not much care for such a description of her remedies.

And the idea of Mr. Myles as a "sweet biddy" almost made her laugh. But she chose to volunteer nothing at all.

"I believe the direction is clear, Mr. Wenfield. Thank you so much. We could spare no one here to take it yesterday."

With protests that the service was very much his pleasure, Perry Wenfield then managed to capture and kiss her bare hand, which Anne considered too high a price to pay for Mr. Myles' convenience.

When she returned to his room, her patient's eyes were closed. Ned had already removed the writing box and placed it on the side table.

Anne paced before the window, considering Perry Wenfield's astonishing offer. The proposal was certainly not her first, but she had thought the possibility of further offers remote. Mr. Wenfield, it seemed, had not heard that Miss Whyte of Wiswood would not marry.

At some slight sound, she stopped pacing and looked to the bed. She thought there was something new in her guest's gaze, but she could not identify it. He looked concerned—but equally appraising.

"Have you injured yourself, Miss Whyte? You are limping."

Chapter Three

I have been limping for many years, Mr. Myles. I'm surprised you've not noticed before." She stopped pacing and moved to the foot of the bed.

"I have scarce been awake these two days, Miss Whyte. And every time you enter and exit this room, you carry heavy trays with yet more elixirs. The limp is hardly noticeable."

"I believe it is more pronounced when I am fatigued."

"Has speaking with Mr. Wenbridge fatigued you?"

"Mr. Wen*field* has not fatigued me. Racing up and down stairs to convey your message might well have."

Myles thought her clearly in a bit of a pother, though whether he or Wenfield had brought it about, he hadn't a clue. What he did know was that Wenfield was the tenant at Hollen Hall; he had recognized the name and heard the saphead yelling it outside. As a tenant, Wenfield was causing the Duke of Braughton some degree of trouble, though Myles had yet to uncover its nature. Myles had carefully directed his note to Phipps at a Pooley Bridge pub rather than to the Priory, so that upon its delivery, Phipps might not unwittingly betray him.

Myles did not want Wenfield to know that Braughton's son was visiting in the area. That would not do. Nor would letting his hosts, who knew Wenfield in some closer, personal capacity, know that he was Lord Hayden. Hayden himself had been on the verge of revealing it; now he determined to remain 'Mr. Myles' for the rest of his stay, which he would make as brief as possible. As soon as Phipps could come to him, he would remove to a room in Hawkshead—above a stable, if need be.

He admitted to some feelings of regret at these plans as he observed his hostess.

"I apologize for sending you up and down stairs. I do appreciate your efforts. Do tell me, though, how you injured yourself?"

"An accident. When I was seventeen. I was not quick enough to remove myself from the path of a carriage."

"You are lucky to be alive."

She tilted her head as she gazed steadily back at him. "I am aware of it, sir. And now—we were interrupted earlier, when you asked me to call you something other than Mr. Myles."

"Yes." He paused, then smiled. "You must simply call me Myles."

"I will not!"

"'Tis quite a privilege."

"Oh, no doubt, and one frequently exercised. If you cannot bear to be addressed properly, I shall simply call you 'sir.'"

Staring at the obstinate set of her chin, Myles considered it more likely that Anne Whyte would choose not to address him at all. But the danger had at least been averted, and in any event, he would not be staying much longer.

"What did Mr. Wensley have to say?"

"Mr. Wen*field* is none of your concern."

You are wrong there, sweet, Myles thought, and he smiled at her. "That he should leave you pacing in front of the window is evidence of some discomfiture. I blame him as the cause."

"He surprised me, that is all. 'Tis disturbing."

Immediately Myles asked sharply, "Your maid was with you?"

"Oh! Oh, certainly. You misunderstand me. Quite—quite the opposite. Mr. Wenfield made me an offer."

"*Wenfield?*" For some reason, he was at once aware that his head ached unbearably. He would have welcomed some of that tepid willow bark tea. But as he rubbed his forehead, she ignored him.

"Why should you be so astonished, sir? Yesterday you were surprised that I was unwed. Do you retract your compliment?"

"Never, Miss Whyte. I am not surprised that the man should offer. I am surprised that you should consider him."

"You do not know him!"

"I know that he lacks a sense of propriety; he makes calls before noon. I know that he yells at his servants. And—I suspect that he is much too old for you."

"Too old for me? Why, he is but one or two years older than I! That you press me about this is not such good form in *you*, sir. I suspect you have been spoiled."

"*You* certainly spoil me."

"I effect a speedy cure, that you might regain your health and be up and about."

"And on my way."

At that she stood silently and watched him.

"I shall bring you some tea," she said shortly, and she left the room with only the slightest sign of a limp.

Oh, well done, Myles, he thought with considerable self-reproach. He should never have remarked on her disability; he should certainly never have pried into the reason for Wenfield's visit. But having done so, he was forewarned. This caller was the son then, not Braughton's tenant, but he would still carry a tale were he apprised. And he might be involved in the father's affairs.

Myles thought it suitable punishment that Molly brought his tea and that the stuff was nearly cold. As soon as he'd finished what little might relieve his headache, he closed his eyes, effectively dismissing eager Molly. The silly girl looked at him as though he were something to be eaten. He shuddered at the thought but soon drifted off. And when he next woke, it was dark.

Anne Whyte sat next to the bed, her face and bright hair lit by the flickering glow from a single candle.

"I thought I would check on you," she said softly. "But you need your sleep." As Myles' blurry gaze moved beyond her to the silhouetted figure in the doorway, she added, "My father has returned. He will see you tomorrow."

Myles was so sleepy he could not keep his eyes open. He wondered if she had supplemented the tea. But how could he accuse her? His headache was gone, and he had not coughed for hours.

When he next woke, it was morning. The manservant, Ned, settled a cup and small pot to the side of the bed.

"You told me you preferred coffee to tea, sir. So Miss Anne sent this up."

"Is there anything in it?"

Ned looked confused. "'Tis just coffee, sir."

Myles propped himself up to take the cup and sniff the brew. She was too clever for him. It smelled, and—as he found— tasted, just like coffee. He then asked that Ned help him wash and dress. The exercise left him exhausted, and he returned to a chair by the double windows, where he had an excellent view of part of the lake and, in the distance, the Langdale Pikes. The day looked sunny and mild. Myles lent his head against the chair's high back and dozed.

"Ned told me you had insisted on leaving bed," Anne Whyte said as she entered the room with the servant behind her.

Myles managed to rise from his seat, but as he stood, he had to cling to the chair back. "*Je suis faible*," he muttered.

"Weak you certainly must be, but I did not know you were also French, sir."

"Your pardon. Sometimes I speak it without thinking. My *grand-mère* is French." Myles noticed idly that Anne Whyte was taller than he'd anticipated; she topped his shoulder. "You speak the language?"

"I understand some of it. There is little opportunity here to do more than read it. I cannot claim any great facility with languages, though I have found the study of Latin useful in my herbal work."

Reminded, Myles looked at her suspiciously.

"What did you put into the tea last night?"

"Valerian," she supplied promptly; she had the gall to smile at him. "'Tis a mild sedative." She met his gaze directly. "You needed the sleep."

"I should rather know what I am taking."

"Did you taste the whiskey in the tea as well?"

"*Whiskey?*"

"Ah, here is my father. Papa, this is our guest, Mr. Myles, who, I am glad to say, is looking very fine this morning."

Myles attempted to erase his scowl as he bowed to the other gentleman. The movement left him lightheaded; he grasped once more for the chair.

"Pray take a seat, Mr. Myles," Anne's father said kindly. "I fear you are not yet well."

"I am much improved, thanks to your generosity, Mr. Whyte, and your daughter's skill."

"She is undoubtedly skilled. But you must not let her bully you."

"Papa!"

Mr. Whyte grinned. He was not a large man, but his posture and manner were relaxed and confident. He had a pleasant face rather than a handsome one. Gray liberally sprinkled his brown hair and he was tanned, as though he spent a good deal of time out of doors without a hat. Myles liked him on sight. But the only feature he appeared to share with his daughter were his intelligent, expressive gray eyes.

"When you are able, you must come down to my library and select something to read. I'm surprised Anne has not brought you any books."

"She has not neglected me, sir. I have scarcely been alert to read." He shot her a quick, accusing glance. "I expect my manservant here soon, though, and hope to impose on you no more than another day."

"One day! It is your choice of course, Mr. Myles, but Anne tells me you need at least three more days of care."

"There is a fine line, sir, between submitting to care and being bullied."

Mr. Whyte laughed.

"So there is, young man, so there is." His daughter, Myles noticed, looked composed but chilly. "We must find that line through negotiation. Perhaps your stay might be a bit longer than you propose, and a bit shorter than we would wish."

The invitation was most graciously extended; Mr. Whyte had a way with words. Myles bowed to him again and once more sought the support of the chair back. He conceded that his host might also be sensible.

"I shall bring you something to eat, Mr. Myles," Anne said as she accompanied her father out the door.

Myles collapsed into the chair. His weakness, the inability to move about as he desired, the recurring headaches, all made him fume. But Anne Whyte had thought he looked "fine." What did that mean?

Again she sent him porridge with port syrup and whatever it masked. Myles indulged in less of it than he had the previous day. He wondered if Miss Whyte's secret remedy was to keep her patients perpetually bosky. He sat up to eat but soon surrendered once more to a longing for bed. Ned helped him undress and crawl back under the covers, but before he could sleep, Anne Whyte delivered another compress for his chest and two volumes from her father's library.

"Father thought you might like something to occupy you."

Myles opened the cover of *The Odyssey.* Inside the book, Mr. Whyte had tucked a brief, handwritten note: *Lest you believe yourself a captive of Circe.* As Myles smiled, he folded the paper. The bookplate named EVERETT WHYTE and included a scrolled Latin phrase.

"I confess my Latin is rusty," he said, showing her the flyleaf. "The truth shall make you free?"

"*Veritas vos liberabit.*" She smiled. "I fear so."

The second volume was a history of relations between the English and the French. Myles looked to her with one eyebrow raised.

"You told him my grandmother is French."

"I must have," she said. "I did not think it a secret." She paused. "What did Father say in his note?"

"Now that *is* a secret." Myles smiled at her obvious frustration. "What did you mean earlier, Miss Whyte, when you claimed I looked 'fine'? Do you suggest I am looking well?"

"You look better, sir, than you did two days ago. But you must concede you are not yet well. I meant, with my comment, only that . . . only that your coat is very fine. You dress well. You were wearing the newest trousers. We do not often see such—such—"

"Foppery?" Myles suggested, recalling that in town there were those who called him "His Resplendence."

Anne Whyte's cheeks turned pink. "Not at all," she protested. "Just that your clothes are excellently tailored and of a most superior quality. You must be prosperous, sir."

"Should you like to know my income?"

The pink in her cheeks deepened charmingly. Myles had to believe himself much improved, because he had the instant urge to kiss her.

"If you reveal it, sir," she said with spirit, "I shall be compelled to demand payment for your stay. And I should much rather not."

"You might have any payment you please."

Her eyes darkened. His tone, or his look, must have alerted her to her danger. *Something is very much wrong with you, Myles Trent,* he thought as she quickly excused herself. He could imagine what his *grand-mère* might say: *She is not Molly. She does not play the game.* And with the echo of Grand-mère's scolding in his ears, he turned his relieved attention to *The Odyssey.*

He was asleep when a tap at the door woke him. In this household, he had rarely heard a knock, perhaps because his door had most often been ajar. As Myles opened one eye upon Ned, who had been dozing in his chair, Ned sat up guiltily, looking as startled as Myles felt.

"My lord . . . above!" Phipps' recovery was quick, but Myles still sent him a cautionary glance. The valet stood in the doorway, clasping two large satchels. Myles hoped they contained some fresh linen and another coat. "Sir," Phipps tried again, "I have come."

Myles dismissed Ned and signaled Phipps in.

"You made good time," he said. "You met Miss Whyte below?"

Phipps shook his head. "Mr. Whyte sent me straight up. I did not meet his wife."

"Not his wife, his daughter." Myles watched Phipps as he placed the satchels on a bench. "How did you travel?"

"I had Perkins drive me as you suggested. He has put up in Hawkshead with the horses and awaits word from you. I came on with just these"—he indicated the bags—"in a hired cart."

"Good man. I shall wish to stay here through tomorrow, but then we must take ourselves off."

"You look much better, my lor—sir."

"Miss Whyte might very well cure me, were I to give her the chance. But I must move on." This did not appear to make much sense to Phipps; indeed, it did not seem entirely reasonable to Myles. But the decision had little to do with reason.

"Where shall I sleep, sir?"

"There's a pallet. Ned and the youngster, Tim, have used it. There's another manservant—Simmons, I think—a cook, and at least one maid, Molly. You must watch yourself with all of them, Phipps. I am Mr. Myles of London, an estate agent on the way north to Ullswater. You might say I travel quite a bit, but seal the lips at more. They'll think you merely proud."

Phipps nodded. "Might I get anything for you now, sir?"

Miss Whyte, Myles thought instantly, and as instantly tamed the thought.

"Hand me that robe, if you would, Phipps. And I find I am a bit hungry. See if the cook might send me up some broth. But settle yourself first."

When the valet had gone, Myles attempted to get out of bed on his own. He was still weak, but the headache and fever had at least temporarily deserted him. He stood at the side of the bed and tightened the dressing gown about him. Then he walked slowly to the windows.

Clouds had moved in. Indeed, the Pikes were obscured and the nearer fells misted with rain. Even amid the gray, the grassy fields looked luxuriously green, almost too fine for the sheep. The woods and shrubs were coloring with the season, hazels and berries ripening where they draped the network of sensuously curving stone walls. Just below the window, beyond a tumble of box and late-blooming roses, Myles could make out the corner of a garden. Anne Whyte, her bright hair covered by a bonnet, was at work tending her herbs. Myles heard someone call her from the kitchen, no doubt to determine the dosage of medications in his requested broth.

He watched her until she turned the corner of the house. Her limp was indeed slight, but it was there nonetheless. He could not believe the imperfection had dissuaded potential suitors. But most men, as he well knew, more readily tolerated flaws in character than in conformation.

The thought of Anne Whyte being so dismissed incensed him.

She and Molly were shortly at the door, bearing a basin with another compress and a tray with his meal. Phipps took the tray from Molly, who eyed him as roguishly as she eyed every man, and set it on a table before the window.

"I did not realize you were up, Mr. Myles," Anne Whyte said, apparently at a loss as to what to do with her infernal compress.

But she seemed accustomed to seeing her patients in informal attire.

"I felt it time. I cannot stay abed forever. And I believe we might dispense with the compresses." That had her lips firming. Myles knew his height, if nothing else, often lent him an advantage. But she was not intimidated.

"You are resolved to court a relapse, sir," she said. "But I shall not let you." She handed the basin to Molly, who curtsied and left the room. "The compress will be ready once you've finished your meal."

"You are a most managing female."

"And you, sir, do not know what is good for you."

Myles sighed. "You sound like my *grand-mère*."

"She scolds you?"

"In blistering French. She struggles for revision, you see." Gesturing Anne to the seat opposite, he sat down by the windows. Phipps brought a blanket for his lap. "My *grand-mère* wishes to improve upon my father—in me."

"You must tell her that she had greater responsibility for your father. If she is dissatisfied, the result is her own fault."

Myles' gaze narrowed upon her. "That is precisely what I have told her."

"And how does she respond?"

"Grand-mère says, '*Avoir ce q'un désire*—'" He caught her eye. "She tells me, 'To have one's wish, one must forget logic.'"

Anne laughed. "I imagine I would like the lady."

Myles surveyed her amused face. Her complexion was still fresh from her outing in the garden. She was, Myles thought, as lovely and lively as any of the ladies Grand-mère admired and commended. But the image of two such stubborn women confronting each other had him raising a brow; at such an encounter, he should prefer to find himself in another room.

"I believe the compliment would be returned." Despite her inquiring look, he did not explain his smile.

For a minute, she watched him eat. After some days of consuming very little, he ate slowly but with appreciation.

"Do you like the broth, sir?" she asked at last.

"Very much. How have you amended it?"

"Why should you believe it 'amended'?"

"Because it seems you must add some of your magic to everything, Miss Whyte. Even the simplest broth."

"It is one means of dosing you, sir. Since you must question *everything*." As Myles conceded that with a smile and the smallest shrug, she confessed, "The broth is flavored with some thyme and parsley and marjoram—little more than the most everyday cookery might require."

"And the bread?"

She tilted her chin. "The bread has crushed garlic."

"*Garlic?*" He kept his countenance and pointedly broke off a piece of the roll. He had partaken of something similar in Italy, after all.

She rose from her seat. When he moved to rise as well, she stayed him.

"If you do not find it appetizing, pray do not persist. But I think it most appealing, and it may do you some good. Now, please, excuse me. I shall be back when you have finished."

Myles consumed more of the bread than he would otherwise have done, at no cost to his taste. But as soon as he had put the tray away, he had Phipps find him the tooth powder. He refused to be reeking of garlic, even if Anne Whyte wished it.

He had planned to attempt the stairs that afternoon, but bed drew him once more. He was already half-asleep when his hostess returned with her compress.

"Father hopes that by tomorrow you might join us for supper," she said. "I have told him I shall do my best."

"And I shall try as well, Miss Whyte."

She felt his forehead, and smiled. "You are progressing, sir."

"Thank you," he said meekly.

"Do you find your breathing easier?"

"What am I to say, when you have just swaddled me in another layer of gauzy treatments?"

One brow rose indignantly.

"I do not ask as a courtesy, sir. I ask because you might articulate your symptoms better than I might gauge them."

You are a proud lass, he thought. But he said,

"My chest, my breathing, is much relieved."

Still she did not smile. She told Phipps when and how to remove the compress, then made to leave.

"Miss Whyte, please forgive me. I have been cross."

"Your spirits improve, sir. You are recovering."

"You must think me a most intemperate man."

"Aren't you?"

He laughed, which again made him cough. She turned with concern, to hand him another horehound drop. Only this time, as she passed it to him, he grasped her hand as well as the lozenge and kissed the tips of her fingers.

She did not look shocked. She did not look anything in particular. Myles thought she must not have realized what he had done; he was, after all, coughing. When she at last spoke, her voice sounded distant.

"I must leave you now, Mr. Myles. It looks as though 'twill rain, and I have work in the garden. I shall send up some tea to help you sleep."

Let her think, then, that by saluting her hand he had merely wished to thank her. *Let her think gratitude had prompted him to overstep.* Anne Whyte might have her pride, but the Marquis of Hayden had his as well.

Pride, it seemed, had to sustain him for almost twenty-four hours. In all that time he did not see his savior again, though Phipps and Ned informed him that she had come to see him twice while he slept.

The next afternoon, considerably refreshed and stronger both in body and in purpose, Myles bathed and dressed. He sat up to eat another meal of broth and rolls. When he noticed his hostess in her garden once more, he commanded Phipps to help him slowly down the stairs.

Myles leaned more heavily upon the banister than upon Phipps, yet still the valet looked dubious.

"My lor—sir, you are still weakened by your illness."

"Which is why you must go out this afternoon, Phipps, and procure us a carriage—the simplest contraption will do—to transport us to Hawkshead tomorrow morning. I must leave, but—deuce take it!—I cannot seem to order my own limbs."

"Yes, my—sir."

Myles walked across the center hall, toward the corner where Anne Whyte's garden was located. Off the hall, what had perhaps been at one time a small breakfast parlor was now a very busy dispensary—a beehive of counters, shelves, cupboards, and one long worktable. Drying herbs of all description hung on racks from the ceiling or were spread upon screens. Open shelves boasted bottles of vinegars, oils, potions, and preserves. The precious still for making decoctions appropriated one corner. The table held several sizes and styles of mortars and pestles, knives, spoons, graters, and chopping blocks, as well as a single oil lantern. There were bowls and flasks, cups for measuring, a scale for weighing. In front of the fireplace, where a few flames flickered, a single rocking chair looked as though it was rarely occupied. Light from one large eastern window reached only the hall end of the room. The rest seemed to be kept purposely dim.

Along one counter, a library of books with well-worn spines announced *Dictionary of Medicinal Herbs*, *The Compleat Herbalist*, *Compendium of Herbs and Spices*, *Herbal Practice* . . . Myles stopped reading. The room smelled most prominently of cloves. But that was probably because, through a large door to the side, Myles could see the kitchen, where Cook was preparing dinner. Myles could not recall the last time he had actually *seen* a kitchen.

He stood, oddly entranced, at one end of the long worktable and looked down its length to the glass door and the greenery beyond. On what looked to be an increasingly overcast day, his doctor dutifully continued her harvesting. Myles supposed he ought to turn about and restrict his exercise to the stairs, but he could not.

He walked to the glass door and opened it upon Miss Whyte's garden.

Only a narrow walkway of slate separated the house from half a dozen raised beds, defined by intersecting gravel paths. At first everything looked a wild confusion; Myles was used to clipped turf and hedges, to graceful *allées* of limes and oaks, to Chas' elegantly satisfying vistas. He was acquainted only with order, not this vigorous jumble of foliage and scent.

A stone wall divided the garden from the pastures and fields surrounding the rest of the Whytes' home. A narrow lane, which Myles took to be the road to Hawkshead, ran on into a barely visible settlement about five hundred feet beyond a gate, where a gnarled greengage tree stood sentinel. Late roses and many colorful hips clung to the wall, as though for protection from the overwhelming sea of herbs. Myles found curious comfort in recognizing the roses.

"I am pleased to see you outside, sir," Anne Whyte said easily. "You had no difficulty on the stairs?"

"Phipps—" Myles said, looking around him. He had forgotten about Phipps. The man must have stayed behind in the hall.

"Your Mr. Phipps," she smiled, "could not have carried you. You are stronger."

"Yes." He thought her eyes, out here in her garden, looked even more changeably gray, as though they reflected both the sky and the variable color of the growth about her. He had never before been so fanciful.

She turned to resume her clipping, which entailed holding long stems upright and snipping them off at a strategic spot, the determination of which defied Myles' understanding.

"I attempt to gather as many cuttings as possible today before it rains. And it does threaten to rain once more."

"Might I help you?" He surprised himself with the offer. He could not remember ever rousing himself to help with such a task. "Though you are tall, I might still reach some of these here in the center." He demonstrated his reach. "Do permit me. I must make recompense in some fashion, Miss Whyte, since my arrival here delayed your work."

"'Tis the purpose of this *work* after all, sir, to be applied to healing, in just such a case as yours. You mustn't feel you owe me."

She was always quick to confound him. He chose to fish for the next stem and say nothing.

"You have no gloves," she said.

"As you do not prune roses, I shall not be harmed." He looked at the lacy foliage before him. "Is this something I have swallowed?"

Her laugh delighted him. "You hold *Achillea*—yarrow. And yes, I have given you some in your tea, for fever."

"Perhaps I ought to ask if there is anything in this garden I have *not* swallowed."

Again she laughed.

"Many things, sir. You have been ill. But you can hardly harbor every ailment at once."

"I thank God for that." Again he looked over her garden. "Is there any system? A plan?" He could tell that she smiled, though she wore a bonnet and looked down.

"You think my garden a jungle."

"It certainly *thrives,* ma'am."

"The plan, such as it is, is mapped in my mind, sir. I study the requirements of an herb, then provide what it needs. If something thrives, as you say, I do not move it. If it struggles, I try it elsewhere. And for most, I attempt to maximize the sun, which is no mean goal here in the lake country, as you know."

"But you do not arrange your plants alphabetically or by their application? How many have you?"

"In truth, I have never counted! And I arrange them most broadly. Here you see many types of lavender. There, the mints, the sages, thymes: Betony, chamomile, elecampane, pennyroyal, rosemary . . ." As she started to list them, he smiled. "Many herbs have a number of applications. Something like this *Artemisia,* wormwood, might treat fevers or sprains, or even an infant's colic, but it always must be grown and used with caution. In general, I choose the most direct remedy I can, with the fewest ingredients. Then I might determine whether a particular herb has served. 'Tis simpler." She caught his eye. "You think *me* simple."

"On the contrary. I think you impressively empirical. Knowledgable and inquiring. Your methods may be simple, but the thought behind them, and the effort, is anything but." He surveyed her fresh face. "And withal, you are so kind, so generous, that I have come to think you quite the saint."

Her countenance looked precisely as it had a second before, but something had changed. He wondered by what sorcery her face conveyed her disappointment with the comment. He had meant to compliment.

"You plan to leave," she said, reading *him* only too correctly.

"I must. I am walking, talking, and eating. Little more is required of a man, after all."

"You may be *coughing* again soon as well."

Myles shrugged. "'Twill be nothing to speak of. You have cured me of the worst. And very quickly, I might add."

Again, that clear gray gaze seemed to look through him.

"Given time, I might have done more." She paused and glanced away. "Father will insist that you stay for dinner tonight. But for now I shall make you some syrup to take away with you." She walked ahead of him. As they neared the threshold to her herb closet, a sleek gray and white cat crossed their path, rubbing first against her skirts and then, astonishingly, against Myles' boots.

"Is he yours?" he asked.

"I believe so. But you must ask him." As Myles laughed, she called "Elijah!" but the cat continued on his way around the corner of the house. As they entered her sanctum, she added, "He will stalk along now to the doorway, out of the rain, and beg a scrap from Cook. When we have guests, he is not permitted in the house." She turned to him. "For some, Elijah is an affliction of his own." She removed her bonnet and asked, "Have you had any difficulty with cats, sir?"

"I have had no difficulty with cats, Miss Whyte, because I have had no dealings with cats."

"You do not like them."

"I do not know them at all—nor chickens, doves, or a host of other domestic fauna. I claim to know horses rather well. And I have on occasion patted a dog."

"'Tis clear you were not raised on a farm."

Only a much too extensive one, Myles admitted silently. Struck by that irony, he simply smiled at her.

Through the door to the kitchen, they could see Phipps seated at a table, speaking to Cook and a maid, who had supplied the manservant with a mug.

"Should you like something?" Anne asked. "Some tea?"

"It is never possible to get something as plain as tea here, Miss Whyte. I must always be dosed."

"You did not object to your coffee this morning."

"And what was in the coffee?"

"Chicory." She turned from him to fetch a pint bottle of dark liquid from a shelf. "Father likes it. And I am not *dosing* my father."

"I stand corrected, ma'am." Myles sensed he was beginning to tire. Frustrated that he could not stand and speak for even an hour without feeling fatigued, he straightened his shoulders. A gentleman did not slouch in the presence of a lady.

"Do take a seat, sir. I am not accustomed to having someone loom over me as I work. You might easily upset my measurements. I cannot answer for the consequences."

He sank gratefully into the rocking chair by the faltering fire.

"Only the smallest step between a poison and a remedy. Is that not so, Miss Whyte?"

She looked over at him in surprise. "That is very true. I wonder how you come by such wisdom?"

He had no wish to answer her. Such wisdom stemmed from too much experience. But she gazed at him so inquiringly that he volunteered, "Hair of the dog, Miss Whyte. 'Tis true of spirits."

"Yes, I see." She concentrated on the portions for her syrup. To avoid focusing on the mesmerizing motion of her hands, he looked about him.

"This is certainly no jungle," he remarked.

"I am glad to hear it. 'Tis even alphabetized," she added mildly, "though in sections of which you would no doubt disapprove." As he started to object, she ignored him. "Sometimes I believe I know this room so well, I might find what I need in the dark. Should I ever be ill, I might direct someone else to my own remedy."

"I do not care to think of you ill, Miss Whyte."

"Nor do I, I assure you! But we are, none of us, invincible."

He supposed he had thought himself invincible in many ways—if not in the matter of this cough. He supposed he still thought himself invincible. He had so much, controlled so much—and might anticipate more. But no, he was not quite invincible. There were things beyond his control. Myles was reminded of it as he watched his hostess warm some freshly cut herbs between her fingertips before dropping them into a vial. A peculiar lethargy stole over him. Yes, he was tired, but still awake and attentive, as though under a spell. Anne Whyte was an enchantress.

"You are a witch," he said aloud, only to have her smile at him.

"The local one, certainly. There are much more powerful witches in Lancaster and Carlisle."

He laughed. "You do not counter the charge?"

"I do not take such imaginings seriously, sir. There is a bit of magic in any healing, and most assuredly a great deal of faith, but what you see here is mere application, not alchemy."

"*Cela ne fait rien.* 'It makes no difference,' lass. However practical you think it, 'tis sorcery to me."

"If I were truly a sorceress, Mr. Myles, why would I not cure my own limp?"

For a second he met her gaze. There was something more to her question than mere playful argument. Did the leg trouble her more than she admitted? Did it pain her? He had, oddly, not given her limp another thought.

"Because it does not trouble you," he decided. "You do not think of it. Or if you do, you likely make a virtue of the flaw. For—so disguised—you would never be thought a witch."

She laughed. "My reason cannot bear it, sir! I cannot be angel, saint, liar, and witch at once! Now let me boil this for you in the kitchen, where Cook will resent my intrusion upon her dinner preparations."

"I fear I must rest before dinner."

"You needn't apologize. Rest is something I cannot bottle, yet surely 'tis the most effective remedy of all. And I must warn you—at dinner, my father is unlikely to spare you. You will need all your strength at conversation to satisfy him."

Yes, Myles thought, *and I must keep my wits about me—over Wenfield and this clever miss.* He took his leave of her and returned pensively to the safety of his room.

Chapter Four

Mr. Everett Whyte, country gentleman, kept an excellent table for a guest and a stranger, with a choice of dishes calculated to meet the special needs of that recovering stranger: savory consommé; delicate lake trout; roast pork with rosemary, cloves, and applesauce; boiled potatoes; and freshly baked bread and rolls, the latter from the manor's own oven. Myles could not have eaten a quarter of what was offered to him, but under the watchful eye of his hostess, he strove to sample everything. He wished her to be at ease with regard to his departure.

He himself felt increasingly loath to depart. In the candle and lantern light, Anne Whyte appeared to glow, like the enchantress he had determined her to be. To keep himself from staring, Myles repeatedly surveyed the dining room.

It was intimate and well appointed, with attractive paper and a blazing hearth. Over the mantel, an expansive landscape painting portrayed a hunting party upon the magnificent fells. Mr. Whyte laughed as he confessed that, even after years of inquiry, the location depicted remained a mystery to him.

Cumberland, most especially its attractions and its history, was the main topic of conversation during the meal. Mr. Whyte, not content to be merely a gentleman of leisure, had tasked himself with compiling a record of that history. He took many short trips to gather material. He was, he claimed genially, in the midst of writing his third volume.

He also shared his daughter's direct manner.

"Sir, I notice your appetite. I hope my daughter's ministrations prove salutary?"

"I believe your daughter has done more, Mr. Whyte. I believe she has cured me."

"Cured you? Hmm. I've the highest regard for Anne's skills. Indeed, I think that—were she a man—she would be admitted to the Royal Society!" At this, his daughter blushed prettily and demurred, but he continued. "I confess to finding yours a most prompt *cure,* though, sir, even given the potency of Anne's powders and potions. I understand you were carried in just Sunday evening."

"I was. But I have been ill in this manner before, and never have I felt so cheery in so little time."

Miss Whyte examined his cheery features from across the table.

"I am pleased that you are encouraged, Mr. Myles. But I believe I've told you that a cure may not be possible."

"My daughter is too cautious, sir," her father said. "Pray do not let her discourage you."

"Miss Whyte would only ever be an inspiration." Myles looked to her. He could not seem to keep his gaze from drifting back to her. As she returned his regard, she spoke to her father.

"You know I have never cured flummery, Father."

Her father laughed. Myles was curiously pleased by the ease between father and daughter.

"Have you suggested to Miss Whyte, sir, that she compile a book of her own—a book of remedies?"

"I have done just that, Mr. Myles, but she will not comply. I believe my Anne Amelia withholds her knowledge so that everyone seeking a cure must come in person, as a pilgrim, here to our home."

"Oh, hush, Father! You know my objection to such a project." She looked across at Myles so frankly, so openly, that he nearly held his breath. "In a history, if something should be printed incorrectly—a date perhaps—or if someone should dispute an interpretation, a reader might simply say, 'Mr. Everett Whyte is incorrect! I disagree!' But should a printed remedy hold the slightest error, a reader might not survive to protest!"

At that, Myles laughed along with her father, but as he started to cough, Anne's smiling features instantly sobered.

There was something sweet in her concern. Myles told himself he did not want her to worry for him—and convinced himself she merely studied him. He sipped his wine, which calmed the cough, yet could not curb his desire to look at her.

"You have been troubled with this cough on other occasions, I hear, Mr. Myles," his host said. "What was its origin?"

"When I was sixteen, sir, I spent a prolonged period under water due to an accident, an incident involving my brother. I trace the problem from that time. But as I've relayed to Miss Whyte, I've no notion as to what initiates subsequent bouts."

"And how many have there been?"

"This is the fifth. Each time, I fear my past catches up with me. But I have been spared the life of an invalid—it is, thankfully, not the consumption—and I find I can contentedly conduct my affairs with little reference to the malady." As he wished to abandon the subject, he diverted. "I am most interested in your history of the district, sir. Why did you not lend me your titles, instead of the books you did?"

"You are my guest, young man. And you are ill. I had no desire to make you more so!" He laughed at himself. "No, I think it is fare best sampled on a sturdy stomach. Anne is always my first and best reader, but also my severest critic. And she has told me my tomes are not for the fainthearted."

"I have said no such thing, Father. You mustn't use me as an excuse." She looked to Myles. "He is too modest. He would never assume your interest."

"I assure you that I *am* interested, Mr. Whyte."

"Then before your departure tomorrow, I shall burden you with the first two volumes." The mention of that departure temporarily suspended conversation. Myles did not quite like to be reminded of it, and Anne's face, so laughing and gay a moment before, now looked too carefully polite.

"Do tell me, sir, with regard to your third volume, does it include our present day?"

"It does indeed."

"And how do you find sentiments in this region? These are difficult times."

"The 'times' here are much as they are in the rest of the nation.

All is changing," he observed. "And if you are traveling here for any period at all, Mr. Myles, you shall confront the many problems for yourself. It has not been sufficient to win a war, preferable as that must be to the alternative. What do we do with the peace? We do not reward the sacrifices all have made. We were one country, but now, I fear, no longer. The fervor applied to defeating Bonaparte has not been directed anew. 'Tis not how I wish my 'history' to end." He shook his head.

"I suspect we face further difficulties."

"Our difficulties are already jostling us, sir! There is much discontent—about the lack of work, the price of corn. The rents and taxes keep rising. Parish relief grows. Farmers default on their debts. Some—not here, but west and east of here—have lost their land. Returning soldiers have no pensions." He glanced to his daughter and seemed to calm himself. "It is a fact that living here on the land, one is immediately aware of the slightest alteration in circumstances. To put it most bluntly, we've a decided want of prosperity in all things. You'll hear arguments that 'tis worse in the towns. But at least there, a man might continue to feed a family."

"I have heard proposals," Myles said slowly, "to ease the adjustment. To lower taxes, or eliminate tithes—"

"Either would be welcome, sir. But who is forwarding these proposals? Who would implement them? The opposite is the reality. There have been—dare I say it?—many royal missteps. And between administrators, in London and even here in the parish, and the working people, lies such a depth of distrust that—I regret to say—any proffered adjustment is treated with suspicion. Here in Cumberland, the enclosures did not bite as hard as in the south, where all the disruptions still fuel resentment. But that parliamentary imposition—based, no doubt, upon that body's collective wisdom—increased skepticism everywhere. The current situation is untenable. If the larger landholders would lower their rents, *that* might bring an immediate relief. But we are only told that they themselves have debts. And so on up the ladder! Yes, I say the peace has come at quite a cost. And the perception of London, for all its bustle, and of our leaders, for all their travel to Vienna and Paris, is that they lack all sympathy and will be slow to change."

"Many do not have the opportunities—or I should say *take* the opportunities—to learn of these problems at first hand. The owners of the land do not work it."

"Then they shall find themselves reading petitions soon enough," Mr. Whyte said grimly. "Once the snows curtail their country sports!"

"Father—"

"My own interest—my hope," added Whyte, glancing briefly at his daughter, "is not in politics, but in agriculture. Scientific innovations must improve the lot of us all. But everywhere the question is the same. What do we choose to preserve? Farmers fear that anything new threatens their livelihoods rather than increases chances for wealth. No"—he again shook his head—"there is too much suspicion."

"Not among those who know their neighbors," Anne said. "You have mentioned many times how those who work together have no opportunity to think ill of one another."

"And so it is, lass. But—ah! Mr. Myles, do not tempt me on the vexed subject of parliamentary reform!"

"No doubt you believe in such reform?"

"I do, sir. We mustn't adhere mindlessly to our forebears' antiquated ways."

"And yet there is an argument to be made for continuing virtual representation, for leaders who think of the country as a whole."

"They do not do it," Whyte insisted, then paused. "Is that what you believe, sir?"

Myles sensed the challenge in the inquiry. "I cite the argument. It is not mine. Nor is the House of Commons my venue." He took a sip of wine and swallowed his slight deception. "I've a notion, sir, that if our economic woes were to be united with reformist urges, we might confront considerably more upheaval."

Whyte eyed him. "That is a most keen observation, young man. And something I hope we would avoid, or see only locally, as we did with the machine breakers. In my view, though, the government would be most unwise to *assume* such a connection, or to anticipate it. I have heard too many rumblings about the prospect of maintaining soldiers in our midst, and some here even in this district start to whisper of informers and spies. A rational man—a humane man—might be forgiven for thinking our leaders are likely to judge this incorrectly and, being afraid, choose suppression."

Anne was looking to her father with concern.

"Mr. Myles will deem you a radical, Father."

"I doubt his thinking is so simplistic, lass." Nevertheless, his host sat back and visibly relaxed. "I dwell on this a great deal more than I ought, Mr. Myles," he said, "because I see the problems and wish them to be solved, calmly and reasonably. Our countryside is still the lifeblood of the nation, despite the growth of the mills and towns and ports. Yet our government seems determined to drain it rather than harness it for the good. Perhaps you might tell me what the logic is in London, sir."

"I regret I have not been in London, sir. What I have heard since June is all of negotiations for a new treaty for France, and of Vienna's Final Act—of those efforts to keep Europe itself peaceful."

"Precisely so! Liverpool and Castlereagh will curry favor with foreign princes while stomping honest Englishmen beneath their boots."

"There must not be another war."

"Certainly not. But neither must there be a revolution here at home. Surely 'twould be better to welcome *some* change than to imprison one's own people?"

"Father!" Anne now looked alarmed. She glanced apologetically across the table at Myles. "When Father returns from one of his journeys, his views are always freshly exercised. People tell him of their concerns, you see, and he feels the frustration of being unable to *act* for them."

"Anne needn't apologize for me, young man. I am aware of how *exercised* I become. 'Tis no doubt the result of reading too many newspapers and not enough of the scriptures, or so my late wife would have said! I shouldn't wish my speeches to make you uncomfortable."

"Not at all, sir. You do little more than report your observations, which I have no reason to doubt, and relay opinions, which may or may not be your own. You are a historian, after all. You choose to assess. I can only appreciate the insight."

Even as Everett Whyte tilted his head in acknowledgment, he watched Myles with a curious expression on his face, an expression that led Myles to wonder whether he might have sounded too circumspect. He was used to being discreet, avoiding taking sides and never revealing more than necessary. He was used to being consulted, to dealing with facts rather than sentiments. He was not used to braving a passionate country gentleman at his dining table.

He was on the point of telling the Whytes just who and what he was when Everett Whyte startled him.

"Anne says you are an estate agent, here to visit some properties."

"Yes, sir. North of here."

"Which properties?"

"Hollen Hall, for one. And the Priory at Ullswater. I might go on to Keswick Manor."

"All the Duke of Braughton's."

"Yes."

There was a pause. Myles looked across at Anne's widened eyes.

"You keep high company, sir," she said.

"I am here *for* him, not with him," Myles said with some irritation. "As a matter of fact—"

"You must be glad you are not with him, sir," her father interrupted sharply, "as Wenfield has been saying Braughton is a good deal of the problem in these parts."

Myles firmed his lips as he looked down at his plate and the untouched apple tart. Beneath the table his fists clenched.

"Would this be the Mr. Wenfield who called here yesterday?" he asked.

"Wenfield here yesterday?" Mr. Whyte looked to Anne. "Is this so, Anne?"

Miss Whyte's cheeks were pink. Perhaps there was something there after all. Myles was thankful he had been cut off in mid-sentence. If this woman—this *girl*—were intending to marry so slanderous a fellow as Wenfield, Myles had no wish to favor her.

"Perry Wenfield came to call yesterday," she said. "'Twas not important."

"But what did he want? Did he wish to see me?"

"No, Father."

Given her heightened color, Myles wondered at her father's obtuseness.

"The Wenfields, as you might know, Mr. Myles, lease the extensive manor and farm at Hollen Hall, one of your destinations. They have resided there for some seven or more years."

"Indeed," Anne said, "after such a time, it almost seems theirs."

"But it is not," Myles said shortly.

"No. Of course it is Braughton's."

Her chin was high. Her father, observing her, remarked, "And now Perry Wenfield threatens to offer again, does he?" As Anne merely nodded, Everett Whyte sighed. "I used to take students here, Mr. Myles, to tutor for university. I had to stop when it became apparent that they were more interested in pursuing Anne than in preparing for their examinations. As she only grows lovelier, I cannot have them back."

"Papa!" She glanced across at Myles. "My father stopped tutoring when his history consumed him. I assure you he tells you a fiction."

"You deny that your sister ran off with one of my pupils?" Whyte demanded.

"That was *Sarah,* Father. I never had any wish to do the same."

"And why not?" Despite the demand, his tone was playful. "What is wrong with marriage, might I ask?"

"Nothing is wrong with it, sir," Anne countered in the same spirit. "But if you wished me to marry, you should not have made other provision for me." Despite her swift defense, her cheeks still glowed. Myles sensed the two were used to teasing each other on the topic.

Her father's eyes were twinkling. "My dear, you can do better than Perry Wenfield any day. What has he to recommend him, after all—apart from riches, a fine person, and a speedy curricle?"

"Well—" Anne smiled. "He promises to teach me to play silver loo."

Myles laughed. Loo had to be the tamest of games, yet Anne

Whyte spoke as though playing it were a most exhilarating prospect.

"Are you a card player, sir?" Everett Whyte asked quickly.

"Indeed, on occasion. Whist is my preferred game."

"And have you lost a great deal at cards, Mr. Myles?" Anne challenged him.

"Lost a great deal? Yes, I have," he responded, while silently adding that he had *won* ever so much more.

Both the Whytes looked disapproving.

"You will never better your station in life, Mr. Myles," his host advised, "if you gamble large sums. You must build some fortune, else you will find it impossible to keep an establishment, to have property of your own, or to marry—unless, of course, you have married money or intend to marry money."

"I am not married, sir." Myles smiled, thinking that these country gentry were decidedly frank. "Indeed, I have recently attended so many weddings, I find I would scarcely have had time for my own." For some reason he dared not look across at Anne. "My cousin wed last year and my brother only this June. Two good friends have followed them to the altar, and another promises to do so shortly." Indeed, he thought it likely his next letter from Knowles would bear news of a betrothal to the lovely Natala.

"And what has soured you so on matrimony, sir?" his host asked.

"You mistake me, Mr. Whyte. I am not 'soured' on marriage. All those I mention seem happy enough. But I do not share the romantic notions of your lake-country poets. Marriage is a game in which I do not hold a hand. Others are likely to arrange mine for me, in any event."

Anne Whyte was looking at him with puzzlement. He might have told her then and there that he was Hayden, and still she would have failed to understand. Few did.

"Good heavens, young man!" her father exclaimed. "Your creed—apparently of resignation, of sacrifice—is one I have never encountered, even among the most violent church reformers!"

Myles laughed—and coughed. This time he could not stop. From across the table, Anne Whyte passed him one of her prepared drops, which he eagerly grasped and downed. Within seconds it had soothed his attack, but Myles determined it best to bring the evening to an end. He wished to hear from Mr. Whyte just what Wenfield had said of the Duke of Braughton, but Anne made no move to leave the gentlemen to a separate discussion. And her presence, apart from distracting him, made an honest inquiry regarding Wenfield impossible.

"I cannot trespass on your hospitality any longer, sir," Myles said as they rose from the table. He had noticed Miss Whyte's gown as they came in to dinner and now, again, admired its beauty, which so pleasingly suited her own. But when he attempted to meet her gaze, she looked away. "I intend to remove to Hawkshead in the morning."

"I do not know how to interpret such a desire," Whyte said affably, "coming so soon after our meal! You needn't rush away, Mr. Myles. You are welcome to stay until your cough has disappeared."

"You would only wish that *I* should disappear long before that occurrence, sir!" He shook his head. "I cannot take such time. Though some of your daughter's lozenges would certainly ease my banishment."

"I dare not give them to you," Anne explained. "There is too great a possibility you would take them more frequently than you ought."

"You believe my discipline that weak, Miss Whyte?"

"I believe you still unwell, sir, and people who are in pain do not regulate themselves."

He bowed to her. "Once again you speak only wisdom, ma'am."

Her father had been observing them.

"But you intend to stay in Hawkshead some days, Mr. Myles?" he asked.

"As your daughter notes, I mustn't hurry a recovery. I might delay my arrival at Ullswater until next week to no ill effect. But if you would kindly lend me your gig tomorrow, sir, I would send it back from the village."

"I shall drive you, Mr. Myles," Anne said.

"Surely that is not necessary."

"My daughter often drives in to Hawkshead on a Friday or Saturday, to see her friend, Mrs. Sprague, over the weekend," Mr. Whyte said. "She will simply go in earlier tomorrow."

"There is nothing unusual in it," she assured him.

"I am quite capable of driving."

"How can you say so? You needed your man's help to descend the stairs!"

"That is not driving. I am not proposing to walk to town, or to scale Scafell."

"This is another argument you cannot win, sir." Mr. Whyte patted him on the shoulder as they moved into the hall. "Anne insists on driving you. And I must say, given your unpredictable health, that I think it a good idea."

Anne had walked ahead of them and now stopped to have a word with the manservant, Simmons. Myles leaned to Whyte and asked very low,

"What does Perry Wenfield say of the Duke of Braughton, sir? I think I had best know it."

"I understand 'tis not *Perry* Wenfield, but his father, Titus, who says such. Titus Wenfield claims Braughton has been forcing the farmers to shorter terms for the land. So that he might continue to raise rents beyond all bearing, higher than any others in the district. All this, in order to obtain even more, to do with as he pleases. I do not believe the claim, as Braughton already has so much. But these wealthy, absent noblemen—"

"The charge is false," Myles interrupted firmly. "'Tis ludicrous."

"You will have trouble convincing anyone otherwise, Mr. Myles. Ah, lass. Our guest says good night." Phipps had appeared behind Simmons. The Whytes must have had a separate wing to house servants. Myles realized that he still had no clear conception of the size of his host's establishment.

He said good night and made, he thought, a respectable showing in mounting the stairs. Part of him wished that his hostess would bring him another compress, but he guessed that she would not. With his revived strength and alertness, he sensed that she was as aware as he of a new constraint between them, and that she, at least, would be wise enough not to test it.

Anne had sent some tea up to him during the night, in case he had any difficulty sleeping. Phipps had collected the tray at the door, which was for the best, since Anne had not been at all certain she wished to see her patient. She thought her new hesitance most peculiar, since she was quite certain that she did not wish for him to leave. And she had been used to entering his room without a qualm.

Her father called her into his library in the morning.

"You must let this creature go, my dear," he told her, examining her face too closely. "There is something here that troubles me. Oh, nothing untoward," he assured her, reading the dismay on her face. "He is obviously a gentleman, and of some considerable means, I should imagine. His countenance, his manner, his *mind*—all speak of consequence. And Braughton! Perhaps it is only that connection that lends him such presence. But he is too quick, and prudent as well. Our conversation at dinner was one that he controlled, not I. Indeed, I feel I said too much—at my own table! He is used to discourse at a most challenging level. I should not like to cross him."

"All this, Father," she exclaimed, "from a man you scarcely know! I thought him merely reserved."

Her father was shaking his head.

"Perhaps with *you* he has been less guarded. I would not know how to interpret that. Illness lowers a man's defenses. But take care, my child, not to discover more than courtesies in his behavior. And do not pretend to misinterpret me."

"I shouldn't wish to, Father."

"That is all to the good, then, my dear."

So warned, Anne saw to her own minor packing for her stay with the Spragues and put up a small bundle of syrups and lozenges for Mr. Myles, who had a quick breakfast in his room. While he took leave of her father, Anne cooed to the mare, Bess, and supervised the loading of the gig. Myles' man, Phipps, assured her that he might ride easily in the back above the luggage. He weighed, he told her with considerable pride, very little.

When Mr. Myles appeared outside, he was again dressed in the immaculate garb that so strangely intimidated Anne. For the first time he wore a greatcoat, against the chill of the late-October morning, and a hat hid most of his light hair. But his gaze was as acute as ever as he first acknowledged Anne and then turned to checking the harnessing of the mare.

"I assure you, all is in order, sir," Anne said with some heat. "We well know how to get about here in the country."

"I do not doubt it, Miss Whyte. And I apologize. But 'tis my nature to check"—he paused—"everything." Despite having been ill, he easily swung himself up onto the bench and nodded to Phipps, who less agilely clambered up behind. Anne waved to her father, who stood watching at his library window. Then they started.

"I don't believe I have said a proper good morning to you, Miss Whyte." He was surveying her, from her beribboned straw bonnet and best cloak to her gloved hands. She thought his gaze amused. "Good morning."

"Good morning, sir. You slept well?"

"Very well, thank you. I suspect I was once again dosed in my tea."

Anne concentrated on driving the gig.

"I do not know how I shall weather the coming days without my medicines," he continued easily. "I have become so used to your considerate additions."

Anne patted the small bundle beside her. "I have packed you some syrups and lozenges for your cough. But should your fever return—"

"I believe I am past that, Miss Whyte. You mustn't worry. I thank you for the remedies."

"And what did my father have to say this morning?" she asked, hoping her parent had not gone so far as to treat their visitor like another Perry Wenfield.

"I believe most of the conversation was on my side, Miss Whyte, which was as it should have been, my being so greatly in his debt—and even more so, in yours."

"You mustn't feel that you owe us anything, sir."

"But I do, and I shall feel so for the rest of my days."

When Anne glanced briefly at his profile, she found the set of his features somewhat severe—as she had thought him on first viewing him and not as she had seen him since, jesting and teasing.

They were taking the road, passing south through the village of Wiswood, then around the foot of the lake and up the west side of the water to Hawkshead. Though the route was longer, it was wide enough to support a carriage. No trip of three miles could take very long. But her passenger observed the few buildings along their way with interest, and Anne spotted at least two faces peering out at the carriage from the safety of the curtains. She hoped at least to be spared any quizzing regarding her companion until the following week.

"Your mare has a good gait," he remarked. "What is her name?"

"Bess."

"Bess! My dear Miss Whyte, all carriage horses deserve more respectful appellations than that! Surely you might have done better?"

Despite her resolve to be merely polite with him, Anne had to smile.

"I did consider another name, sir, because she seemed so proud and fine. But then I feared she might not stoop to service."

"And what was the name?"

"Duchess."

He caught himself—on a laugh or a cough, she could not determine—but as she turned to him, he waved aside her concern.

"Have you ever known a duchess, Miss Whyte?"

"I am told I met the Duchess of Braughton when I was ten years old. She was visiting in the area, at a fete. But I scarcely recall anything other than my own terror." As she laughed, he looked to the side.

"Terror," he muttered, "would have been appropriate."

"Do you keep a horse, Mr. Myles?"

"Yes. I ride and drive a good deal."

"Do you? Even when you must travel such distances to visit estates?"

He frowned. "'Tis not unheard of for passengers to spell a coachman on occasion. But more often I drive for the pleasure alone. In fact—if you will permit me to mention it, Miss Whyte— on this hill you might let your mare have more rein. You make this harder for her."

Anne drew a quick breath.

"I wonder why it is," she managed tightly, "that all gentlemen assume they know best how to drive a carriage? Next you shall claim to be a Four-Horse Club member!" She thought his small smile abashed.

"I cannot speak for 'all gentlemen,' Miss Whyte, only for myself. I regret that you have been plagued by ill-judged advice in the past. But if you will simply try giving your Duchess more rein, you shall see."

At first, Anne refused to comply. But her nature was to experiment. Once Anne did relax her hold on the reins, Bess settled almost instantly into a steadier, easier pace.

Anne said nothing. She refused to say anything. Mr. Myles seemed absorbed by the view of little Esthwaite Water, obscured by a thick cover of mist despite the sunlight and clear blue sky. Shore birds were noisily waking in the shallows and reeds beside the road.

Though he did not look at her, Anne was too aware of him, of his shoulders, his booted legs, his warmth.

"Do you stay in Hawkshead every week, then, Miss Whyte?" he asked. In the distance, they could see the first slate rooftops and squat white chimneys above the trees.

"Oh, no! Perhaps once a month, at most. The church at Hawkshead is one of the largest in the county, but the size of the congregation scarcely warrants a resident vicar. So Mr. Sprague and Vera—my friend, Mrs. Sprague—live in Ambleside and come out early on Fridays, returning after matins on Sundays. Sometimes they stay for a week, as they plan to this next. My father and I usually come in on Sundays only. But on occasion I like to spend more time with Vera. You give me an excuse, Mr. Myles."

"I shouldn't think you would need an excuse, Miss Whyte. Or do you in truth come to see Mr. Wenthorne?"

With considerable effort at calm, she replied, "I do not come to see Mr. Wen*field,* sir, and it is most unmannerly of you to suggest it." She coaxed Bess into a trot, so that the journey might end more speedily. When Mr. Myles drew his coat collar up higher against the quickened breeze, Anne felt not one whit of remorse.

Hawkshead was little more than a hamlet, but the wagon roads passing through from the Windermere ferry and points west and north, and its picturesque setting in the tranquil valley, lent it the quality of a destination. The whitewashed and many half-timbered buildings clustered about a sloping square, where a number of wagons appeared to be setting up for an impromptu market. Anne drove on to a house just below the hilltop church. Though it was early, the Spragues would have come out even earlier from Ambleside, as Clement Sprague was always most conscientious about meeting with his parishioners. Indeed, a slim curl of smoke rose from the chimney. The Spragues' young servant, Nate, came out to take Bess' head.

Mr. Myles descended in one step. He held up a hand to help her down. They had not said a word to each other in five minutes. But as Anne placed a gloved hand in his, she could think only of how he had stolen a kiss upon her fingertips just nights before.

Knowing that her face flamed, she concentrated on the small parcel she clasped in her right hand.

"I suspect you will not need these now, sir," she said, still looking down, even after she had reached the ground, "but they are some insurance should you find yourself—"

"Floundering."

"Yes." In some relief she was able to look up with a smile. "I know you feel better, but you mustn't tax yourself."

"Which is why I linger here before continuing north. You must believe, Miss Whyte, that it is not my habit to delay so."

She nodded. "And where will you stay?"

"Phipps and I"—he looked about him, to find Phipps standing with the satchels in the street—"have not yet determined it. But we shall find something to suit."

"There is one inn, the Beckside, farther along the road, and rooms above the pub at the Blue Duck. But you should probably prefer the inn. I ought to have stopped there first."

"Do not trouble about it, Miss Whyte." He still had hold of her hand. She was regretting the last minutes of their ride; she was regretting ignoring him, now that it was so apparent that they must part. But if he were in town this weekend, she was more likely than not to see him. Indeed, she had relied upon it, having last stayed with Vera only two weeks ago. Again she felt too warm, though the morning was a crisp one.

"Miss Whyte, I cannot thank you enough for all you have done for me. If I might ever return the favor, you have only to contact me."

"And where shall you be found, sir? Pooley Bridge?"

For a second, he looked at a loss.

"At the Priory there, yes. Even if I am traveling elsewhere, I shall hear of it." As he raised her gloved hand and lightly kissed it, Anne swallowed.

"I shall pray for your good health," she said.

"And I for your happiness." He released her hand and turned to take her satchel from Phipps.

"Oh, you needn't!" she protested.

"'Tis nothing. Hardly enough to tax me." He gestured her ahead of him toward the stoop. Vera herself was opening the door.

"Why, Anne! You are so very early! We have been here only this half hour. Have you—" Vera's smile faltered as she focused on the tall stranger behind her. As Anne reached the stoop, she grasped Vera's hands and kissed her lightly on one cheek. But Vera's gaze was on Mr. Myles, who tipped his hat and made an elegant bow.

"Vera, this is Mr. Myles, who has been recuperating with us this week. He felt well enough to come on to town today. Mr. Myles, my friend Mrs. Sprague."

"Ma'am." As he smiled pleasantly, Vera looked dazzled. Indeed, Anne knew *herself* dazzled—by the smile, the hair, the eyes, and the easy assurance. But when she next glanced at her friend, Vera's expression was one of puzzlement.

"Surely, sir," she asked, "we have met before?"

Chapter Five

I've not had that pleasure, ma'am." Certainly Mr. Myles did not act as though he had ever met Vera. His smile was still as open as before. He did not pause before replacing his hat. "Perhaps I remind you of someone."

"Yes. Yes, that must be so. But do not stand here on the doorstep! Please, come in."

"I cannot stay, ma'am. Thank you. As Miss Whyte knows, I must seek lodgings this morning."

"But you might stay here with us!"

Even as Anne tried to catch Vera's eye, to signal that such an invitation was extravagant and certainly not *her* wish, the intended recipient of such hospitality was shaking his head.

"You are too kind, Mrs. Sprague. The temptation is great, I assure you. But I mustn't. I cannot." Turning to Anne, he bowed again. "Miss Whyte." He stepped back to where his man waited with the luggage. Young Nate had already taken Bess and the gig around to the stables. Anne watched Mr. Myles lean to grasp, over his man's protest, one of the heavier bags. He did not look back as he strode easily on down across the cobbled square, toward the road and the river, his valet trailing behind him.

Anne felt the slightest bit numb.

"Anne." Vera pulled her inside and quickly shut the door. "*Tell me.*"

"He is—" she began. She did not have a word. "Vee, I am not at all certain I know what I am about."

"I should say you must know very well what you are about!"

Vera's look was amused. "Oh, Anne, he is *lovely*. And the way he looks at you! I doubt he is even aware of it. How delicious!"

"You are too sensible to speak so." Anne moved on into the tiny entry. She had forgotten to hand him his parcel. She placed it on the console table and slowly removed her bonnet. "The man has been ill."

"I cannot believe *that* gentleman has been ill a day in his life! Apart from being a bit too pale—I must believe that *this* time, Anne Whyte's cure has truly proved miraculous! Dearest, why could you not have sent me a note? And to arrive here so early, and on a Friday!"

"I truly did not know I would come on here, Vee. Not until late last night. When he suggested he might drive, I knew that he shouldn't. That I must come."

"I am very glad that you have, of course. And Clem will be delighted. He's already gone out, to Tate's. Our most capable blacksmith, Booth, set the leg for Tate, as you have no doubt heard, and Mr. Albright has tended him. You'll want to see Tate as well, I know. But not just now. We must have a talk first. Have you had your breakfast? Come have some tea with me."

Anne settled in the tiny parlor, in which almost every surface displayed some shade of blue, Vera's favorite color. Vera herself was not the most immediately striking of ladies, but her lively, intelligent nature lent much attractiveness to her person.

Anne could only ever view her fondly. Vera had been friend, sister, and absent mother at once. Her humor and good sense had attracted shy Clement Sprague when he first came to Hawkshead five years before. They had subsequently obviously, and most charmingly, shared much attention and affection. Their parishioners had benefited greatly from the couple's kindness.

"You thought you had met him before, Vee?"

"Just for a moment. There was something, perhaps his hair, that made me think it, but clearly not. I refuse to charge so exquisite a gentleman with a bad memory! Nor do I wish to consider *myself* so forgettable."

Anne laughed.

"There," Vera said. "You look much more the thing. For a

moment, I thought you might topple to the floor. You mustn't become ill yourself now, Anne, for none of us would know how to restore you."

"*You* would not, Vee. I might have more faith in others. From you, I should wish only for sympathy."

"I can well believe that! For any potion of mine would certainly make you worse rather than better."

Anne smiled. Vera's skills lay in needlework and embroidery and in unfailing kindness, not with preparing anything more complicated than tea.

"Now tell me, how did he come to you?"

Anne relayed when and how Mr. Myles had been delivered to her.

"He was scarcely conscious, and Tom Shanks had to hold him upright upon Jamie Ballard's cart when they brought him. I'm certain good Mr. Dilly or someone here in town paid Jamie to do so, for Jamie's not known for lending a hand. Then Father's man Ned and young Tim helped me nurse him, because Father was away—"

"You are compromised," Vera suggested slyly. "You must marry him."

"You are most droll, Mrs. Sprague." Anne looked to her in exasperation. "Vee, do stop your jesting and let me finish, else you'll complain that I keep everything to myself."

As Vera settled back in her seat, Anne told her of the efforts to reduce her patient's fever and the unceasing application of compresses for his cough. She did not relay her worries for him or anything of the nature of their conversations. Vera listened attentively, then surprised Anne by shrugging.

"Well, if you will not have Mr. Myles—if you think him too much work—perhaps you will reconsider Perry Wenfield. He is to be in town this evening for Squire Peabody's dancing."

"A dance here in town—tonight?"

Vera nodded. "To celebrate the birth of his much-desired grandson. We just heard from the Lesters next door. Mr. Peabody wanted the musicians from Kendal, but they have an engagement tomorrow, so they're coming on here today to the assembly room at the inn. The squire has invited everyone in town, and has probably sent to Ambleside and Wiswood and Grizedale—even Bowness and Coniston, I imagine. It shall be a crush, Anne, even in the inn's ballroom."

"But Mr. Wenfield?"

"Ah, you are interested, are you?" She laughed at Anne's expression. "He told Booth he'd be back this afternoon for a repaired wheel rim. If so, he cannot avoid our happy throng. So I am counting on you, Annie, to take advantage of the suitor and the situation at once."

"Why is it that everyone credits me with an interest in Perry Wenfield!"

"Perhaps because he makes so clear *his* interest in you?"

"But you know better!"

"I have not seen you in two weeks, dearest. I should have thought Mr. Myles *better*, but you tell me 'not so.' "

"Oh, Vera!" She wished to laugh but instead protested, "Why are you so determined to see me wed?"

"I would not have said I was, until this morning." She raised her eyebrows expressively, but Anne pretended to ignore her.

"An assembly at the inn," Anne mused aloud. "And yet, I have just sent him there for quiet and rest!"

"You cannot protect him from our sport," Vera charged. "You fuss over him as though he were a child! He is a man my age— or a bit older, if such is possible—though you will think it unlikely that anyone so ancient still perambulates."

"I do not consider either of you 'ancient.' I meant that the inn is bound to be both busy and noisy tonight."

"Mr. Myles appeared to have sense enough to notice the activity. Our good innkeeper is no doubt already engaged in readying his establishment for the event. Or perhaps it eases your mind to consider that if Mr. Myles does not have means enough to afford the Beckside, he shall be snugly slumbering at the pub, or in the poverty of a stable, far from all our hilarity."

"He seemed to have the means."

"Oh? Did you inquire?"

"Of course not! But he keeps a horse. He said he drives often. His clothes—well, you saw them. And his man was always most fastidious, and very deferential." Gazing at the fire in the tiny hearth, Anne found she could picture too easily both Mr. Myles and his devoted valet.

"I see you did not observe much at all," Vera said dryly. "So, rather than dwelling on a gentleman who is by now sleeping soundly and most oblivious to us, might we plan our day? We must leave enough time later, for I wish to help dress you this evening, Anne. Price"—she named her maid—"shall do your hair. And you shall have my mother's pearls."

Anne thanked her. She had brought a good gown for church, one that she would now wear to the dance, but it was not what she would have chosen to wear to such an entertainment, least of all one where there was the slightest chance that *he* might be in attendance.

After their tea, Anne and Vera sorted the baskets and bundles to bestow upon various parishioners: the newly invalided Tate with his broken leg; Mrs. Parell, who had just been delivered of twins; and gentle Nellie Harrington, who had lost both her husband and eldest son at Waterloo that summer.

Once Clement Sprague returned, the ladies were ready to set out on their route and leave him polishing his sermon by the fireside. Though she had stayed with the Spragues many times, Anne rarely coaxed more than two or three sentences at once from the vicar. Vera assured Anne that her husband was always talkative enough when the two of them were alone. This, Anne had always wished to see, for Vera had a tendency to command a conversation.

As they followed the narrow pony tracks to each of the cottages on their route, Anne kept watch about her, as though expecting to encounter Mr. Myles at every turning. Yet she knew the possibility was remote. He was back in town sleeping, as Vera suggested and as she herself had recommended.

Again she scanned the countryside. The day was lovely, warming now in the late morning, with no sign of the rain that had visited them midweek. Only a few low clouds topped the hills, dwarfed by an expanse of fair sky. Gold and copper colored the woodlands. Farmers were busy, hurrying to finish their haying, their industry watched by lazy sheep in the neighboring pastures. From the protection of a low stone wall, a wren scolded the passing gig.

Anne did not recall feeling any of this anxious expectation as she had prepared and plied her remedies or worked outside in her garden during the past week. She had not been nearly so obsessed while the gentleman resided at her father's house. Perhaps simply knowing that he stayed had satisfied her. But she had no excuse for her distraction now; he had not been with them long enough to have become anything like a habit. She must simply reason herself away from this fixed focus.

She congratulated herself upon her good sense, even as she examined William Tate's leg, which was mending, and instructed his wife in the method of infusing a pain-relieving tea. Anne supposed she had become too attached to Mr. Myles as a patient. She had made his recovery a personal goal—a situation not unknown to her—and she had not yet rid herself of that bond. Once she accepted that she was never to see him again, she would be free of this confusion of her senses.

"You are very quiet," Vera remarked as she directed the pony back to the tiny vicarage. "I hope you do not punish me for my teasing."

"I do not punish you, Vera. In fact, I cannot think of any suitable way one *might* punish you, even should that be desired!" As Vera smiled, Anne added, "I was simply thinking that I permitted myself to grow too dedicated to Mr. Myles' welfare. Perhaps because he was a stranger, and alone, and stayed so many days with us."

"That could be, of course," Vera said politely.

"And then, the fact that he is not from the area and might never pass this way again lends a certain—"

"Poignancy?"

Anne shot her an exasperated glance. "*Finality* to the acquaintance. One likes one's friendships to increase and grow. Instead, there is so much—so very much in life that retreats." She consciously stilled her gloved fingers as she realized they had been working restlessly in her lap, and glanced away again toward the hills.

"He did not die," Vera observed mildly, winning another of Anne's repressive looks. "You might see him again."

"That is most unlikely, Vee, as he goes north and then back to London."

"He might pass through again upon returning to London, or he might write to you."

"He could hardly write to *me,* Vee—but I suppose he might write to Father, since Father gave him the first two volumes." She silently debated the odds of such a possibility. If only her father had merely lent him the books!

"And then you might even see him at tonight's dancing," Vera suggested.

"Even if he knows of it—as we've discussed—he truly *has* been ill. A man who was abed just days ago will hardly be tottering into a lively reel."

"No, but he might stand up for something quieter, or simply enjoy watching the revelry in pleasant company."

Something in Vera's voice had Anne turning to her accusingly.

"Vera Sprague, what have you done?"

"I sent Nate with a note for Mr. Myles before we set out, inviting him to join our evening party." She casually urged the pony to an unexpected trot. "Wherever he happens to be staying, Anne, he should have received it some hours ago."

Myles had only stayed because she wished it. He stayed, he thought with some amusement, because she had been so insistent that he must rest. But he intended, after a night in his cramped quarters at the Blue Duck pub, to depart very early the next morning. And in the interim, he walked.

This bout of fever had robbed him of some strength. Myles felt the loss particularly on the inclines, gentle as they were, but he was used to activity and soon adjusted to an easy stride. The few people he encountered were busy with the haying; the greatest obstacle to his peace was one particularly tenacious barking dog. Myles recalled running across fields and slopes much like these when he was a boy. The valley at Hawkshead was more open than the one he had frequented north at Ullswater, but the feeling of the countryside remained the same—at once wild and liberating yet still conveying the comfort of familiarity. Each summit seemed a known character.

He had to wonder what he was about. He, who had always planned so far ahead, now seemed to be living for just one day at a time. Today he would gain some strength. Tomorrow . . . tomorrow he would leave for Ullswater. He would examine his father's holdings there. And he would remove himself from Anne Whyte's company.

A farmer's lad gaped at him from the top of a hayrick. No doubt gentlemen in fine town clothes, when they were to be seen, only walked the roads if they had had an accident—else they would drive the finest equipages or ride the best bloods. But at the moment, Myles had no other form of exercise. He might shadow box, he supposed, once returned to his tiny room. The most devilish thing about being ill was how it left one so far behind.

He stopped to close his eyes and briefly raise his face to the sun. He had never recovered so quickly before; he knew he had Anne Whyte to thank for it. She was sweet, generous, *luminous.* A window had been opened; he had breathed the air.

He had fallen into an idyll, a dream. Little of the past week seemed real, yet he knew he had imagined none of it. The dream was domestic—reassuring and cozy—yet strangely, intriguingly, new.

Again he walked. He was conscious of tempting fate, when he should have felt only what he usually felt—a certain weary acceptance. He had followed—always dutifully, if not with enthusiasm—his prescribed path. At times, perhaps, he had been indolent. He had been prone, as his *grand-mère* so unceasingly charged him, to observe rather than to act. But he had never been inattentive or uncaring. He had aided those he loved. And now, when *he* wanted something, he must break off. He must leave.

His dutiful, if tired, legs had brought him close to the outskirts of Ambleside. The fells loomed closer. Turning to retrace his route, he noticed that visitors appeared to be bent upon Hawkshead that afternoon. Since Myles had been told the weekly market took place on Mondays, he could not imagine the reason for the town's late-week popularity. He kept his hat on his head and his back to any oncoming travelers and attempted to walk as briskly as he had walked out, though his energy flagged.

He tried to recall all he could of Titus Wenfield, tenant at

Hollen Hall. The man had made his fortune as a Liverpool shipping merchant before retiring to the Lakes. Myles thought his own father, the duke, had once described Wenfield as pompous. That Wenfield was fond of grandeur, with perhaps a bit of the pretentious *parvenu* about him, would appear to go without saying, as eight years ago he had leased the grandest of the Duke of Braughton's northern properties. Myles thought he recalled his father fuming that Wenfield was not generous, that—during the first two years of his occupancy—he had failed to treat the tenants to a single fete or celebration, a responsibility incumbent on most landholders and one that Braughton himself had never failed to observe in absentia. Wenfield, for his part, excused himself by explaining that he had no intention of putting down "roots," that he planned to purchase his own property elsewhere in the district and build a residence of his own. But many years had passed, and still he had not done so.

Myles knew nothing of the Wenfield family, except that he deduced a Mrs. Wenfield. The son he disliked on principle.

His pace quickened. Each Braughton property, and there were many, had its own steward, and the stewards in turn reported to several agents—with military exactitude, as his brother, David, described it. The steward at Hollen Hall was Greeley, who had advanced from assignments at two lesser properties near Keswick. Myles assumed the man would not have been so honored had his father not found him more than satisfactory. But perhaps the increased responsibilities had been beyond him, or the duke had been misinformed regarding Greeley's capabilities. Braughton's agent for the northwest, a Mr. Munroe, lived in Penrith. Myles thought an interview with Munroe advisable. Perhaps he must go first to the Two Lions at Penrith tomorrow night.

Two matters disturbed him. First, that letter mentioned to him during the summer, a letter either *from* Wenfield or *about* Wenfield. The letter had troubled his father, though Myles had heard nothing further about the missive. The spring had been a busy one, with David posted to Belgium with the Guards and the subsequent run up to Waterloo. Thus, Myles remembered only that Wenfield had been the focus of his father's concern some months before.

There was nothing unusual in Myles' lack of specific information. Braughton's personal secretary usually kept Myles informed only of general matters. Myles had been far more used to advising his father on pending issues in the Lords than to addressing problems associated with the properties. He was not a farmer; his own interests had centered rather exclusively on London and the larger world. The Duke of Braughton, though industrious and unfailingly careful, had exhibited little flexibility on broader political matters, though he was not immoveable. In consultation, Myles had been edging him, slowly, toward more expansive views.

The second matter, Wenfield's charge against Braughton, incensed him. Though unfounded, such a criticism against a landlord could not be dismissed. The Hollen Hall farmers would not have been complaining without some basis. Myles knew well that farmers compared their situations as frequently as they condemned the weather. They would not have been claiming that their rents were *excessive* unless they were indeed finding themselves hard-pressed in comparison to others around them.

Yet his father had always made a point of liberality; he could afford to. The Duke of Braughton was indeed, as rumors claimed, one of the wealthiest peers in the land. Unlike so many landowners, Braughton had never had to mortgage any part of his estate. In the present difficult climate, few who worked the fields and pastures were doing well, but surely, *relatively,* the Hollen tenants should not have felt ill-used.

Something was very much amiss. His father was far from a negligent man. Though he and Myles had had their disagreements, they shared quick minds and considerable respect. Braughton would never have let specific concerns or grievances continue unaddressed; he would never have risked losing the trust of his dependents. He had no need to press men already tried.

At a shouted "Hallo!" Myles stepped quickly off the road. A high racing curricle sped past, its red wheels hazardously lapping the edges of the track. Myles did not recognize the driver, a hatless young blade with a head of tousled auburn hair. But there was something—the loud shout or the trailing laughter—that reminded him. And at once, though he had been ill abed at the time, he remembered Perry Wenfield's visit to Anne Whyte.

He scowled as he watched the bungler driving at much too fast a pace on this rough track and wielding his whip too freely.

Myles made his fatigued way over the last quarter mile to town. To deal with present circumstances, he might have wished for his usual fitness, but at least there was nothing lacking in his understanding. He and Perry Wenfield could not continue to admire the same lady.

"You shall be ill again, m'lord," Phipps reproved him. The valet had cleaned and tidied the tiny pub room to naval standards. Myles had preferred some peace away from the busy inn. But he still raised an eyebrow at the recognition that his coachman and grooms should now have better accommodation in the inn's servants' quarters than their master had obtained at the pub.

"Not this time, Phipps," Myles told him, sitting to have his dirty boots removed. "And I must make myself fit—so that I might *fit* into my coats."

"Yes, m'lord."

"And you must still be careful, Phipps, to call me 'Mr. Myles' until we leave this place."

"Yes, m'lord."

Phipps handed him a small, sealed letter. Myles broke it open and read Mrs. Sprague's invitation—twice. He knew he should not attend the assembly, but Mrs. Sprague knew that he was fresh to Hawkshead; he could hardly claim another engagement. And were he to plead any indisposition, Anne Whyte would collect him and spirit him away again for another course in enchantment. However much he might desire a repetition, he could not court it.

He was obliged to attend the assembly. But he determined he would arrive late, as was his habit, and he would not dance.

Before settling to rest for the afternoon, he dashed off a response:

Dear Mrs. Sprague,
   I thank you for the invitation. I fear you shall find me deadly dull, but I will join you with pleasure. May I meet you at the event? I shall be late.
                                          Hayden

He stared at the note for a second, then tore it up and began anew. He was most assuredly Hayden; for hours, he had been thinking only of his station and its obligations. Tomorrow, perhaps, he would be *only* Hayden. But for one more evening he must continue to pose as "Mr. Myles."

When he entered the inn's ballroom, Squire Peabody's party had been in progress almost two hours. Fresh from his room at the pub, Myles had taken the opportunity to review the other guests from the corridor and at the side of the dancing. He thought it an irony, that he—who had never walked into a room in his life without wishing to be acknowledged or, more truthfully, expecting to be so—should now desire the opposite. He considered the risk of recognition slight. He had rarely stopped in such a small town in his life, and then only to change horses. He scanned the many guests, at least a hundred of them. Most were clearly gentry from the area, with a few tradesmen here and there among their neighbors, to share a glass of punch in honor of Peabody's new generation.

Myles spotted Anne Whyte as she came down the set, but she did not see him. She was smiling, occupied only by the joy of the dance. He noticed her pale blue gown. For a moment, Myles could not take his gaze from her face. But he was soon startled into doing so, because in the country dance in progress a series of partners helped her through any difficult step by clasping her about the waist and lifting her through.

Certainly no one who had waltzed could object to the move. Most astonishingly, not a single man appeared at a loss as to what he was to do. As a result, Anne completed the figures as smoothly and gracefully as any lady on the floor.

He found the Spragues just steps away from the dancing. Mrs. Sprague looked as though she had recently participated as vigorously as any.

"Mr. Myles, how good of you to join us." Her gaze approved his formal black coat and meticulous, frothy cravat. Despite her warm welcome, Myles could not feel easy with her. He did not forget his momentary panic that morning at her question; she might well have seen him somewhere, anywhere, before. He thought, not for the first time, that there was something very lowering about this deception, however serious the reasons for its continuance.

"My dear Mr. Sprague," she said, drawing her husband, a tall man with frosted dark hair and a cleric's collar, close to her side, "do meet Anne's patient, Mr. Myles."

The vicar extended a hand.

"You are clearly no longer Miss Anne's patient, sir," he said, observing Myles with an approving smile. The smile transformed the vicar's thin face.

"I owe her my health, Mr. Sprague, and possibly my life."

All of them watched Anne Whyte as she moved through the dance. Myles thought her gown and the lustrous pearls quite perfect.

"Do not let her know you believe so, Mr. Myles," Vera Sprague said lightly, "or she might ask for something in return."

"I *have* let her know it, ma'am." His gaze drifted again to Anne. "She might have whatever she will." When he looked again to the Spragues, both were considering him thoughtfully. He realized the conversation was too solemn for such a boisterous event. Vera Sprague, to his relief, smiled.

"Pray excuse me, Mr. Myles. I must speak with my friend, Mrs. Eccles, before the next set."

Myles found himself alone with the vicar.

"Your wife has exceptional high spirits," Myles said as she departed.

"Indeed. My days are an exercise."

Myles smiled. "She and Miss Whyte must make quite a pair."

"They defend our small hamlet, sir, with force of will."

Again Myles smiled. Even with so much activity about, with the music and laughter and light, he could seemingly look nowhere other than at Anne Whyte. With some shock, he realized that many of the other gentlemen in the room, even those with partners, appeared to have the same difficulty.

"They adore her," Sprague said, following his gaze. "Every eligible man in this room has offered for her." At Myles' look he added with a laugh, "I said *eligible*. I had already met my Vera."

"And yet she is not wed." Myles watched her bright hair in the lantern light. He thought she had not yet seen him. "Why do you think that is?"

The vicar shrugged his slightly stooped shoulders.

"You've been told why she limps?" he asked.

"She said a carriage accident—when she was seventeen."

"She saved a youngster's life. Donny Farro was eleven. He'd have been killed."

For a second, Myles could not speak. "Where is the boy now?" he asked at last.

"Off to Liverpool and the docks. He's grown into a big, strapping lad of at least fifteen stone, who could lift Miss Anne—*and* a carriage—with one arm."

"He, also, must adore her."

Sprague turned to him with eyes alight. "I should not have judged you so new to human nature, sir. Donny Farro resents her and the incident. 'Twas to escape any sense of obligation that he ran off to Liverpool."

Myles' eyebrows rose. "She is both healer and heroine, then," he remarked, following her movements once again. " 'Tis quite a burden, for so young a person."

At the vicar's silence, Myles realized that he had sounded just like himself—just like the drawling Marquis of Hayden—cynical and somewhat bored. Yet that was not what he felt. He had spoken from sympathy.

"Your pardon—" he began, but Vicar Sprague shook his head.

"I understand, sir. Perhaps you share similar oppressions—though I would not have thought it."

Myles thought "similar" much too generous. He knew the gulf between Anne Whyte and himself was less one of rank than of heart.

"I am not a hero, Mr. Sprague. And I have been more like to harm than to heal."

"Is that so?" Sprague asked gently.

The question might have invited a confidence. Yet Myles had no intention of sharing such with a stranger, even if a clergyman, and no matter how sympathetic.

In frustration he looked again to Anne. The set was ending; she was curtsying prettily to her partner, a young sprig whom Myles gauged he might vanquish with one word. That he should harbor such uncivil thoughts at such a jolly party appalled him.

"I believe Miss Anne has saved a dance for you, sir, should you have energy enough to claim it." The vicar smiled in encouragement, as a chaperone might, and gestured toward Anne's spot on the floor. "You are a very lucky man."

Indeed, Myles thought, and lucky that the dancers appeared to be setting up for a more mannered quadrille, as he had no fondness for romps and reels. Still, the livelier dances had given half the men in the room opportunity to clasp Anne Whyte about the waist.

He presented himself before her and bowed. The young man he took to be Perry Wenfield had also arrived at her side, sporting a proudly possessive, and equally offended, sneer on his handsome face.

"You would honor me, Miss Whyte," Myles said, "with the next."

"It is yours, sir, if you are feeling well enough?"

Myles merely smiled and inclined his head. He took her gloved hand to lead her into the set. The pearls at her throat were scarcely as luminous as her lovely skin, and the intricacies of her hair might have suited a queen.

Admiring her, he lagged behind on the very first step.

"I did not know if you would come this evening," she said.

"If I had not, you would have chased me down to dose me."

She laughed. "I told Mr. Wenfield that, should you appear, the next dance would be yours."

A stipulation, Myles thought, with a swift glance at the other man, *certain to make any devoted young suitor look as bilious as Wenfield.*

"My apologies to Mr. Wenfell," he said stiffly when next he advanced.

"Mr. Wen*field* is most understanding."

"Apparently he has every reason to be."

"And what do you mean, sir?" Her eyes flashed. Myles was again behind on a turn.

"Are you not intending to marry him? He is, I gather, quite a wealthy gentleman."

"And you think that of me?" The color in her cheeks seemed to deepen the gray of her eyes. But she had admirable self-control. *A much better temper,* Myles reflected, *than my own.* With a gentle arm, he guided her through a turn. "I told you my father has provided for me," she said. "I needn't marry."

"And what is the nature of this 'provision'?"

"Would you wish me an heiress, Mr. Myles?" she challenged.

"And what do *you* mean, ma'am?" As Anne looked away, he said, "I would think it wise for your father to have provision in writing—in the law rather than mere understanding—that is all. Male relatives," he added, "have been known to take issue with such dispensations."

"You sound like a land agent, Mr. Myles."

Thank heaven, he thought, turning from her again, *that I do not sound like a penny-pinching peer!*

"Do not make me laugh, Miss Whyte," he said. "You know that I might cough."

Her smile returned.

"You needn't fret over me, sir. I shall have funds enough."

"But not, perhaps, as much as you deserve." He had not intended to sound so grim, but could not seem to help himself. "I do not *fret* over you. 'Tis merely rational. Shall you have enough for an establishment of your own? What if you were to be ill? And children—"

"Sir!" She recalled him to their circumstances. The subject was too intimate for the cheerful venue. "I appreciate your concern," she said softly, "but truly, you needn't worry." She eyed him most sympathetically. "Perhaps you have felt the hardship of going without?"

He laughed. No one had ever, or would ever, ask him such a question.

"I tend to accumulate money, Miss Whyte. And with it, obligation."

"But you gamble."

"As a pastime only. An entertainment. It has helped me accurately assess risk."

"Yet you admit you have lost a great deal."

"I only gamble what I will not miss. As I have a certain amount of wealth—"

"No doubt growing smaller by the day."

He smiled at her severity and turned with her.

"For someone enamored of 'silver loo,'" he commented, "you must allow yourself envious."

Her laughter followed him.

"I confess," Anne mused when they met once more, "that had I a fortune, I should probably spend it."

"Surely not? You have boasted of the Cumbrian thrift."

At the reminder, she looked charmingly arch.

"Oh, but I should spend it on my friends and neighbors, and keeping up the church, and ponies for the children, and perhaps a school—"

"No bonnets?"

"Perhaps one bonnet. And several parties."

"Parties are great, noisy things," Myles said. "Tedious beyond bearing." Again he caught himself at sounding so superior.

"If you truly find them so, sir, perhaps we should stop dancing." As he smiled, she elaborated, "I should host only lively parties, with only the most intelligent and accomplished and talented and generous people in the world."

"All three of them."

For a second she returned his gaze with an astonished one. Then her lips rose playfully.

"I believe, sir, that I might promise to spend all *your* fortune within a week."

"Most unlikely, my dear," he drawled. The dance parted them. When they advanced together again, he said, "You wear a most delightful fragrance, Miss Whyte. It is not the bay you burned while tending to me, nor my old friend lavender, but something attractively elusive."

"'Tis lemon verbena," she said. "You've an excellent nose, Mr. Myles."

"I thank you. And the rest of me?"

She blushed. Instantly, he knew himself a fool—for seeking compliments, and prosing on about finances—when he had so little time with her. "Forgive me," he said when he again stepped toward her. "I have been too long abed. When I went walking today, I did not feel half myself."

"You must be careful," she said, frowning, "not to attempt too much."

"And so must you. You would oblige me by besting the urge to fling yourself in front of carriages."

"I think I might safely pledge that, sir, as I no longer have the capability."

"No? I should have said you did. You dance extremely well."

"As do you, sir." Her gaze reminded him of his masquerade. "I begin to wonder about your life in town."

"I assure you, I rarely dance." But she did not look satisfied. To divert her, he said, "Vicar Sprague told me about Donny Farro."

"I see." She bit her lip. "'Twas an impulse. A single moment! To so affect one's life—" She was silent for a few seconds. The music approached its close. "Of course, I am glad to have spared Donny, but I should rather not have been set apart."

"You'd have been 'set apart' anywhere, Miss Whyte," he said as the dance ended. Around them the couples were clapping. "Set apart by the quality of your person . . . by the impulse that sent you into the road. There would have been another provocation, another Donny. There might still be. You will always act as you are, Anne Amelia Whyte. And I think you might do whatever you wish to in this world."

He bowed to her, then took her hand to lead her back to the Spragues. She looked very serious. Her eyes were very dark. He suspected that despite his commendation, or perhaps because of it, she fought tears. He felt oddly distraught himself.

Perry Wenfield had attached himself to the Spragues, no doubt to deprive Miss Whyte of any hope of avoiding him. Mrs. Sprague declined Myles' polite offer to dance, claiming she had taken enough exercise for the evening.

"You and Anne seemed to have much to discuss," she observed.

"Miss Whyte is a most engaging partner," Myles assured her. His most engaging partner then introduced him to Wenfield, once again assuming, to Myles' irrational pique, that pretty Perry's consequence was greater than his own.

They scarcely nodded to each other. Perry Wenfield's chin appeared to have risen an inch or two. Myles strongly wished to draw the fellow's cork.

"You've lived in the area long, Mr. Winfield?"

"My parents reside at Hollen Hall, north of here." He did indeed sound as though he, and they, owned the place. "And you, sir?"

"Town."

"Ah!" The fine Wenfield chin wobbled. "I passed you walking on the road today, did I not?" When Myles nodded, Wenfield asked, "No horse?"

Four splendid beauties boarding right here at the inn, thank you very much, you boasting blighter. And at least a dozen more. But Myles said, "Not one."

"I see." Wenfield's lips slid into a smirk. "You stay long, Mr. Myles?"

"I leave tomorrow." He heard Anne Whyte's indrawn breath. "For Penrith and Ullswater properties in the north."

As Wenfield looked pleased, Myles thanked the Spragues. Anne Whyte offered him one gloved hand, which he took firmly in his own.

"We take our leave again, then, Mr. Myles," she said. Her gaze was very clear and direct. Myles wondered if she found this farewell as difficult as he did.

"My respects to your father, Miss Whyte." He bowed low over her hand, resisting the urge to kiss it. "Your servant." He did not look at her again but turned to leave the room. He felt the crowd's attention on him, but rather than accepting it as a given, he wished only to escape. He made his way through the packed ballroom's busy entrance and passed through the corridor. As he stepped outside, into the brisk night air and the narrow passageway leading to the pub, someone cried urgently behind him, *"Hayden!"*

Chapter Six

P urvis?" In the dim lantern light from the inn's side door, Hayden could not see the speaker well, but he thought the round-faced young man walking toward him was Henry Purvis, younger brother of Theodore, one of David's good friends—yet another good friend who had been lost at Waterloo.

"I knew you would remember!" Purvis beamed. "Teddy always said you had the most amazin' memory—for cards not the least of it!" He laughed nervously. "Hayden, the thing is, I'm in a spot of trouble. Is there someplace we might talk?"

Hayden led him silently across to the pub and up to his room. The place seemed even more cramped and close when shown to a guest. He saw Purvis' eyes widen.

"'Od's life! Surely *you* can't be on a repairin' lease, Hayden? Why ain't you over at the inn?"

"It did not suit me." Wishing the interview over quickly, Hayden added, "I was sorry to hear about Ted."

"Awfully hard on the parents," Purvis admitted with a small gulp. "Proud, though, of course, what with Maitland's Guardsmen such heroes." He glanced uncomfortably around the tiny room.

"How might I help you, Purvis?" Hayden asked. "I should rather like some sleep. I'm traveling tomorrow."

"I *thought* those were your bays in the stables! I told Elissa, that's my—well, the trouble is, Hayden, Elissa and I ain't married yet. That is, we meant to be, but one of the horses went lame, so we thought we'd take the ferry and hide out over here across the lake, as the risk was on the road goin' north." His voice softened, no doubt with the frailty of his thinking.

"How did you get here from the ferry?"

"Oh, that! So many were coming on to this do, we just hopped a ride. But now Elissa's worn out, poor thing, and didn't even come down to dance, though the orchestra's quite good, and she loves it so."

"Purvis, I fear we digress. How might I help you?"

"Thing is, I'm run off my legs. Haven't a sou left, Hayden. Not a feather to fly with! Coachman demanded my last to see to the horse. I've nothing to pay for the inn. And Elissa's pennies went to getting us something to eat in Kendal. I've been taking my fill of punch and cakes this evening, I can tell you!" Again he beamed, as Hayden's eyes narrowed.

"Who is Elissa?"

"One of the Birdwistle girls. You know they have five—"

"Yes," Hayden interrupted. "And you could not do things properly?"

"Tried to, truly, Hayden. But the old man wouldn't have it. Birdwistles always have been high in the instep, and even with Teddy gone, I'm still just a younger son. Clifford, you know, inherits. I think you knew him at Oxford."

Hayden had ceased to listen. He had knocked on the door to the adjoining room to summon Phipps, who kept his purse. Once Phipps presented it, Hayden counted out a handful of tenners and passed them to Purvis.

Purvis' jaw dropped. "I say, Hayden, only goin' to Gretna."

"Consider it a wedding gift. And see that you marry as soon as may be. Birdwistle is a stickler—not a man I should like to cross. I've known him some time."

"No, and that's the thing, Hayden. Now that we're *here,* I haven't a clue as to how we're to get *there*. Gretna, that is."

"Hire a carriage." Hayden was herding Purvis toward the door. "Surely someone in this hole—"

Purvis was shaking his head. "No closed carriage. Can't have people *seein'* us, you know. And Elissa's been sniffling the past two days. I shouldn't wish her to fall ill. I wonder—I know it's an imposition, Hayden, but could you possibly take us up?"

"You haven't a clue where I'm headed!"

"With those bays, and the coach—though I know it's not that

rippin' town coach—you *have* to go back to Kendal. All the other roads round here are little more than pony tracks. Or so I'm told. We'll be ever so quiet. You won't even know we're along!"

"As it happens, I do go north, but no farther than Penrith. Your problem will repeat."

"Oh, I won't mind." Again, Purvis beamed. "We'll stop at the Two Lions."

Purvis' persistence decided him. "Take the lot," Hayden said abruptly. "Take the cattle and the coach and the coachman and get back to the turnpike. I'll come with you now to talk to Perkins."

"But why shouldn't we simply accompany you?"

"Because I do not wish to be part of your escapade, Purvis. I can well imagine Birdwistle's penalty for such an indulgence."

"I'd talk to him."

"That doesn't appear to have signified," Hayden remarked. "Now be a sensible fellow and trust to your good fortune. You might impress the future Mrs. Purvis with your ability to provide for her, even if after the fact. But do, pray, invent some tale—for I'd ask that the both of you forget having encountered me."

"Oh, ho! Like that, is it?" Purvis, numbskull that he was, winked. Bridling his annoyance, Hayden brushed past him to open the door.

"Shall we?" He gestured the way out. They slipped down the stairs and out to the alley, then reentered the inn at the back. In the room he shared with the footmen, dour Perkins made no secret of his aversion to serving as unlikely a youth as Henry Purvis, but once told that a lady also required his good offices, he schooled his features. He listened intently.

"Take them up the road as far and as fast as you can, Perkins," Hayden told him. "Change the team at the first decent stables en route. You might tack back to collect them and take them north in stages. Phipps and I shall walk up early Sunday morning to Ambleside, where we shall hire something to take us on. At that, you'd best take most of the baggage in the coach. I've no desire to haul a trunk. With God's good grace, we might have transport by midday Sunday."

"But my lord," Perkins said, "for you to be traveling on the Sabbath—"

"I beg your indulgence, Perkins. It cannot be helped. 'Tis a bit of an emergency." As the coachman hurried out to have the horses put to harness, Hayden turned to Purvis. "If you go tonight, there is less to distinguish you from others leaving this party. And you might make decent time. There is a full moon."

"You're a devil at arranging such things, Hayden. I wish I'd had you to consult at the outset!"

"I'd have counseled you against an outset. The next time you elope, Purvis, make all speed to your destination."

"Right!"

Hayden glanced at him impatiently. "I should like to see your intended, if possible—sniffles or no—to assure myself of her welfare." Even as he asked, he wondered at himself. He really had no need to meet Miss Elissa Birdwistle. But the request was in the nature of a habit; he had been trained to order and decision. Problems seemed to be thrust upon him. Perhaps that was why the friends he chose were those content to relax quietly at the card tables.

And if, by some ill fortune, he should be compelled to wed *Avis* Birdwistle . . .

Miss Elissa Birdwistle looked like all the women in her family, pale and very thin, with a pinched expression to her nose and mouth that was just now exacerbated by the sniffling from a cold, or perhaps from copious tears. She had had the sense to bring her maid with her, which lent some small measure of respectability to the undertaking.

The sight of Lord Hayden, or perhaps his involuntary scowl, appeared to upset Miss Elissa. He knew he was known for a certain detachment, but not, he hoped, for being uncivil. He found it inexplicable that the girl's tears should begin anew.

Thinking of Anne Whyte and of what she might prescribe, Hayden ordered up some tea and a light supper while they awaited the carriage. He spoke to Miss Birdwistle and Purvis as though their plans were indeed *plans,* responsible and deliberate, rather than foolish impulses. He hid his irritation and attempted to grant the two an undeserved degree of respect. Nothing in what the couple said indicated that they had given a moment's thought to their future. Hayden assured himself, however, that they had indeed intended to marry; that seemed to be all they had intended.

"When you return to town, as you will of course—and as soon as possible—you must consult with your mothers," he told them. Hayden knew that both Mr. Birdwistle and Purvis, the Earl of Dalborough, were unlikely to be coaxed quickly into understanding or acceptance. "Lady Dalborough and Mrs. Birdwistle will be pleased to see you so happy," he claimed, though of that he was not at all certain, "and will advocate for you with your fathers. You must have some nature of settlement, Purvis." He glanced impatiently at the still foolishly smiling young man. "Something to live upon. You would not wish your wife to be impoverished."

"'Lissa, poor? I should say not!"

"I shall give you an introduction"—Hayden gestured to his footman, Thomas, who quickly exited the room—"to help you establish yourselves. And then on my own return to town, perhaps in late January, we will discuss what might be done."

Miss Birdwistle looked overwhelmed. Or else, Hayden surmised, she did not comprehend. Purvis seemed incapable of comprehension. Hayden doubted that he himself had ever been so oblivious, even in his cradle.

When Thomas returned with writing implements, Hayden dashed off a letter of credit to his bank and, sealing it, handed it to Purvis. The children might thank him later. He desired them only speeding on their way, and—for his own ill-used and cynical self—the sanctuary of his bed.

With the coach ready, Purvis hurried below to settle the account with the innkeeper. Hayden escorted Miss Birdwistle down to the waiting carriage. The hour was very late, after midnight, and music no longer spilled from the ballroom. A last, lingering number of Squire Peabody's guests made their way out into the night. Hayden and Miss Birdwistle joined them.

Perkins awaited them around the corner with the carriage and the spirited bays. Hayden was aware of the exclamations and compliments bestowed upon the horses as he walked Miss Birdwistle to the side of the carriage.

"I wish you well, Miss Birdwistle. Do not worry. Purvis will see you happy."

"Thank you, my lord. You have—oh, you have made everything so perfect!" Quickly the girl stood on tiptoe to kiss him on the cheek. Astonished, Hayden lightly saluted her hand and helped her up into the coach. "We will call on you *first* when we get to town!" she claimed gaily through the carriage door, as though Hayden had proceeded as he had for the questionable honor of Mr. and Mrs. Purvis' future patronage.

When Purvis came running out of the inn, Hayden tolerated his hearty clasp. Then, with a wave to Perkins, Hayden sent his coach and four onward.

Anne knew he could not possibly have seen her. She and the Spragues were farther along the square and illuminated only by moonlight, whereas Mr. Myles had stood full in the glare of the inn's lanterns. His height, his posture, his dress, had been unmistakable. No hat covered his extraordinary light hair.

She saw him escort the elegant young lady to a carriage pulled by magnificent horses—horses that in the town's tidy lanes looked more appropriate to myth. The lady wore a luxurious fur-lined cloak that must have cost the earth. A maid accompanied her. Anne could not see the lady's face, but she did see her reach to kiss Mr. Myles most familiarly—and his answering salute to her hand.

Anne wished to look away. Instead, she watched the two continue to converse through the open coach door. Only when Perry Wenfield spoke to her did she turn.

"Mr. Myles finds high company," Perry said. He sounded envious. "I wondered about those bays. Did he tell you who the lady might be, Miss Whyte?"

"No," Anne managed. "I did not know he had any acquaintance in the area."

"'Twas condescending of him to grace Squire Peabody's assembly. Myles is clearly used to better."

"Do not be waspish, Mr. Wenfield," Anne said, walking on behind the Spragues. She fought the urge to continue to observe the gentleman, to peer at the coach's occupant, to return to the inn and confront him. Conversing now with Perry Wenfield was a torture.

Mr. Myles owed her nothing. She had told him so. That she should feel betrayed was most irrational. Yet, after their dance and conversation, she had thought that, even in parting, they had understood each other. She had thought there had been some tie. But she had been mistaken.

For the short walk to the Spragues' door, Anne could not hear anything Perry Wenfield said to her. When he took his leave, she felt relief. She now regretted accompanying Mr. Myles into town. She wished to be home with her father and Elijah and her work. She had been foolish to extend her time with her patient. The idyll, she thought, was over.

"Anne dear, you do look tired," Vera said in the light of the entry. "Run off to bed. Have a lie-in in the morning. All our calls tomorrow are here in town."

Anne said good night and left the Spragues speaking together. She welcomed the chance to be alone. Vera was much too observant and much too imaginative. She would know that Anne had been crushed, and by whom, and she would attempt to devise some solution. At the moment, Anne had no heart for solutions. Only one might serve.

She had parted from him with the hope that their paths might cross again, that indeed he might be inspired to *arrange* that their paths should cross again. She had believed that she held his good opinion—and she had granted him hers. Suspecting him lost, even from dreams, was desolating.

She surrendered much of the night's sleep to speculation and woke heavy-eyed. Vera said nothing as they set about the many tasks associated with preparing for that afternoon's calls and the following day's services. Anne always helped. She enjoyed Vera's company so much that even the more tedious occupations passed quickly. And Vera had the sense not to mention Mr. Myles.

By early afternoon, when they set out to visit within the village, clouds had moved in, bringing a persistent, stinging drizzle. Anne and Vera walked with cloaks and umbrellas through the

alleys and narrow passageways. They carried light baskets with
food and favors; Nate followed, carrying more. With the rain,
most laborers had abandoned their efforts in the fields and come
into town. By late afternoon, lanterns appeared in the homes of
those who lived in town and worked the land beyond. The two
pubs and the inn sprang to life with patronage and relaxed spirits.

"Let us just stop at the Blue Duck a moment, Anne," Vera
said as they finished. "I must speak with Mrs. Midgeley about
our harvest fair. We shall be too busy tomorrow morning. I hope
you do not mind."

Anne said not, though the dusk and the damp weighed heavily upon her spirits. At least the pub was warm and full of cheerful talk. With a coin Vera had pressed to his palm, Nate went off
to treat himself to some ale.

Anne dutifully greeted the Blue Duck's proprietor. But as she
and Vera discussed the details of the coming fair, Anne drifted
off beyond the pub's taproom, with its huge hearth and boisterous clientele, and on into the low-ceilinged corridor. A small,
oak-paneled parlor in back served as a local meeting place, one
in which the gentlemen might smoke and converse with their fellows. On glancing in, Anne saw one such group at a round table by
the fire, and, surprisingly, the group included her father.

After a second's hesitation, Anne drew back. Her father had
not told her of coming to town. And there was something both
serious and grim about the gathering. Anne knew them all: Jamie Ballard, Tom Shanks, Thaddeus Digweed, and Po Cowell.
But she hesitated to intrude, all the more so when one of the
men said all too clearly, "I don't want no violence."

Anne slipped to the side of the doorway. Pressing her back to
the cold wall, she closed her eyes.

"No, I shouldn't think you would, Mr. Shanks," her father said
calmly. "That is why you write such a letter, to *prevent* any violence. But you do wish your grievances heard?"

"Oh, aye."

"Tom's right, though. It's a fair way to bein' a threat, ain't it?"
Jamie Ballard asked belligerently. "I'd as soon confront 'em as
send a piece of paper."

"But Jamie," her father interceded once more, "consider the

letter as giving them notice. Perhaps they will surprise you and yield to your requests."

"*Requests?*" Jamie asked. "It's too polite, Mr. Whyte."

"Shall I call them demands, then? And if your demands are not met, what shall you do?"

"Fire the properties. An' maybe some of the stewards as well!"

"As Mr. Shanks says, you do not wish to go that far, Jamie. You mustn't even consider the possibility."

"Sometimes 'tis the only way."

"'Tis never a good way," her father said evenly. "Sign the letter. It is a first step."

"An' how long should we wait then, Mr. Whyte?" Tom Shanks asked. He had a high, querulous voice. Indeed, Anne knew all the men's voices. She quickly assured herself that no one else was in the corridor.

"Why, a few weeks, at the least. A response would be made publicly, of course. Through a notice of a positive result—say, to investigate complaints, or some such. Clearly, we have no way to receive return correspondence." There was rough, rather rude laughter at the joke.

"We're apt to see some public *lashings* in response, sir," Thaddeus Digweed said. He was the eldest of the men. Anne would have considered him experienced and reasonable, above such secrecy. As she would have thought her father . . .

"But if'n we signs it, sir," Po Cowell asked, "won't they jest retal— . . . re—"

"Retaliate, Mr. Cowell? They might. But how much more harm might be done? And think of the example such a response would set for reasonable men! I shall sign it myself as the free Englishman I am."

Oh, Father, Anne thought desperately, *the world is full of many much less reasonable than you!*

"I'll sign as well," Jamie Ballard admitted grudgingly, "but I don't 'spec' no good to come of it—an' maybe some bad. Have you ever known such to work, Mr. Whyte?"

"Indeed yes, Jamie. 'Tis a right of petition we have. If those who govern do not hear from the governed, how are they to know of our distress?"

"Oh, they knows right enough," Tom Shanks said balefully.

"'Taint *your* distress, Mr. Whyte," Thaddeus Digweed added. "Why should you do this?"

"Because I have observed, Mr. Digweed. And I am deeply troubled. If remedies are not sought soon, we shall all be affected by every manner of disruption. We've seen the small holders impoverished, both owners and tenants. You and Mr. Shanks might keep your land with an extension of credit. But where shall you find it? And where shall you go if you lose your farms? Perhaps to the mines or the mills, which will pay you a wage but require you to uproot your families or separate from them. And you are, neither of you, still young.

"So then, gentlemen," he urged. "You asked me to write this letter, as I have done. Shall you sign it or not?"

As the others dropped their voices in a murmur of discussion, Anne attempted to breathe calmly and steadily. A gentleman passed in the corridor from the larger taproom in front. Anne knew she should return to find Vera, but expectation held her still against the wall. And then she heard footsteps from her left, quickly descending the stairs from the rooms above, footsteps that stopped immediately upon reaching the corridor.

Anne looked in the dimness toward Mr. Myles, who hesitated only a second before coming toward her.

"I shall stand with you, of course"—her father's voice came from the room—"and sign as well."

Mr. Myles paused across the doorway from Anne. He glanced briefly into the parlor. In one long stride he was then across the opening and by her side. Anne signaled silence with a finger to her lips.

"We thank ye, Mr. Whyte," Thaddeus Digweed said. "An' it relieves my mind."

"I shall hope it relieves your situation as well, Digweed."

"I still say words won't come to naught," Jamie Ballard growled. "'Tis action we need, so th' owners know what's what."

"You see, Mr. Whyte, Jamie wants blood!" Tom Shanks sounded as though he joked, but Anne shivered, thinking that the sentiment was only too true.

Mr. Myles must have felt her shiver. He gently took her arm and drew her farther along the corridor toward the taproom. Anne did not resist. She had heard enough.

"You should not be here," he whispered.

"I?" She stopped and stared at him. "My *father* is here!"

"And *he* should not be here." Anne felt his attention to her face. "Who are these men?"

"They are—none of them *bad*—"

"I do not ask you"—he was still whispering—"to play St. Peter. Merely to relay their names or occupations."

"Are you a *spy,* sir?"

"For whom would I spy, Miss Whyte?" He moved her away from the parlor, two steps closer to the pub's main room. "You are the one lurking in the passage. Yet it is no place for you. Nor for your father. What I heard was not auspicious." As he still held her arm, Anne shrugged off his hold. They were closer now to the taproom and heard the rollicking noise from its patrons. "Mr. Whyte appears to involve himself in local dissent. He thinks with his heart. It is not wise."

"Of what do you accuse him?" she asked proudly.

One eyebrow rose above his brilliant blue gaze.

"I do not accuse. I merely infer, from what little I overheard. But you yourself were hovering outside the parlor, Miss Whyte. Why? There are those, in these troubled times, who might reach unhappy conclusions."

"You might conclude what you wish," she said coldly.

"He brought you here with him?"

"No. I came with Vera."

"That, at least, is something." He looked very troubled. "Miss Whyte, there are indeed spies about, spies for the crown who equate all dissent with sedition. Who would interpret a plea for understanding—for lower taxes, say—as a threat of revolution. Your father is a rational man, with strong leanings toward reform. I cannot fault him for that. But I fear he goes too far. That is why I ask you, who are these men with whom he meets? If he is not careful, the association might harm him—and you."

"Only if *you* should speak of it!"

"I needn't say a word. Mr. Whyte seems determined to sign documents that would seal his own fate. You must keep him from it."

"I do not rule my father! And why *you* should presume to instruct us—" She stopped, at once recalling the previous night's sighting of this gentleman with an obviously privileged lady. "I forget," she said, her chin high, "that you keep elevated company. And disdain the rest of us."

His lips tightened. "If that is the case, I wonder that I am staying abovestairs here, with a narrow, lumpy bed and a smoking fire."

"You stay here?"

"I do."

"And why are you *still* here?"

"I could not travel today, Miss Whyte," he said, urging her again toward the front room. "But I hope to be gone tomorrow. Shall that satisfy you?"

She did not know what to say. In the past two minutes, her feelings had run the gamut, from surprise, dismay, and anger to jealousy and concern.

"We must find your friend Mrs. Sprague," he advised her softly. "She was in the taproom?"

"Wait." Anne placed a hand upon his arm. Again she noted that his coat was beautiful—the smoothest superfine, not her father's serviceable worsted. She also noticed the surprising strength in his forearm. "I must speak with you."

His face was very close. He held her gaze. "Shall I call upon the Spragues?"

"No. I would speak privately. You attend church in the morning?"

He shook his head. "I leave previous to any service."

"Then tonight. The Spragues retire early, after dinner, because of church tomorrow. I shall offer to lock up and stay below. I shall leave the door off the latch and watch for you."

"Your father does not stay there tonight?"

"He never has." She frowned, thinking that she had not expected him at the Blue Duck this evening either.

"What time shall I come?"

"Perhaps half past nine?"

He nodded, then added smoothly, "Mr. Wenfold will not mind?"

When she did not honor the question with an answer, he placed a palm at the small of her back and moved again toward the main room. He did not enter it with her but continued on out the front door to the square. Anne returned to Vera, who still stood trapped by Mrs. Midgeley and her enthusiasms.

When her father came on into the taproom less than five minutes later, Anne noticed the men with whom he'd been speaking trailing out behind him. But he did not appear uncomfortable or guilty. When she moved toward him, he was obviously pleased to see her.

"I did not know you were to be in town tonight, Father," she said softly.

"I did not intend it, Anne, until I received a note this morning. My talents as a scribe were required once again, it seems."

"By whom?"

"Thaddeus Digweed for one—and Ballard, and a couple of the other small holders."

"To do what, Father?"

He looked surprised. "Why, Anne, surely it is no matter? They send a petition of complaint."

"And why must they call upon you?"

"Because, my dear, they do not enjoy writing. And what they do write is the most rudimentary." He frowned. "It troubles you?"

"It troubles me that you might be used by someone like Jamie Ballard, whom I have never trusted."

"It is not necessary that I trust Ballard. Quite the opposite. He would seem to be trusting me."

"And do you sign this complaint as well, Father?"

"As its author, I take responsibility for it, yes." He tried a smile. "I am surprised at you, Anne. You know that I welcome your views on my writings, on the histories. But it never occurred to me that you should advise me on all my other scribbles."

She blushed at the reprimand, though her fears had not been eased in the slightest. "I am sorry, Father. 'Tis simply that I do not wish you to be . . . to be caught up just now. In associations that are not in your best interest."

"I shall always believe my best interest that of English liberty,

Anne dear. Now, I must ride on home to Wiswood, but let me first escort you and Mrs. Sprague back to the vicarage. When I stopped in earlier, the vicar told me you were out making calls."

So at least, Anne thought in some relief as the three of them walked back, *he did not come secretly to the pub, nor make any attempt to hide what he did there.* But she feared his principled notions would be interpreted as radical, as provocation, and that such a perception might threaten the freedom he treasured.

Hayden anticipated his encounter with Anne Whyte as much as he had anticipated any meeting in years. He knew himself a fool for it; he knew she wished only to discuss her father. But all the same, he recognized the reason for his high spirits.

He had walked again most of that morning and subsequently spent the remainder of the afternoon reading Everett Whyte's first volume. He thought it all the more ironic, then, that escaping from "resting" in his cramped chamber, and in search of a fortifying cup of coffee, he should discover Anne Whyte in such unusual circumstances.

That she had been startled and troubled by her father's activities had been apparent. From the little Hayden had overheard, he thought she had reason for concern. The countryside roiled with resentments and plots, a discontent that the authorities threatened to suppress. Hayden had sense enough to recognize that he could only exercise influence where he held an interest, which was why he had to reach Ullswater and his father's properties. But meantime, he might lend what aid he could to his savior—who, in seeking his counsel, must tolerate his company.

He had his coffee in a corner at the inn. Then, because the place was quieter and more relaxing than the Blue Duck, and likely to have somewhat tastier fare, he ordered an early dinner. While he awaited it, he read an old copy of the *Chronicle*.

"So you remain here in Hawkshead, Mr. Myles." Perry Wenfield stood before him wearing a many-caped coachman's coat, which Hayden was tempted to inform him had been *passé* some years. Wenfield repeatedly slapped a riding crop against one of his corduroy-clad thighs, the motion less threatening than indicative of the younger man's temper, peevish and punitive.

"I note that you also remain here, Mr. Winfell," Hayden said easily.

"I visit with Miss Anne Whyte."

"Do you? And where is *she?*"

"Why"—Wenfield looked disconcerted—"she stays with her friends, the Spragues."

"How fascinatin'." Hayden again turned his attention to the newspaper.

"Look here, Myles," Wenfield said. "I think you ought to know that Miss Whyte and I—that we are engaged."

Hayden looked as blankly upon the puppy as he could. He knew she would have told him. Despite all his teasing, she would have told him if such were the case. Unless she had accepted Wenfield just last night, and *that* was why she had asked him to call—to tell him she had accepted the nodhead.

Hayden managed a small smile.

"My felicitations," he said. "Had I known of your betrothal last night, I'd have congratulated you."

"Yes, well, we did not know last night. That is, Miss Whyte does not wish it generally known. Not just yet."

"Ah!" Again Myles smiled. "The Spragues do not know?"

"No."

And I would wager Anne Whyte does not know either, Hayden thought. He greeted the delivery of his meal with more than the satisfaction of appetite. Perry Wenfield could not be as close to Anne Whyte as he claimed. He was all pride and pomposity. "Won't you be my guest for dinner, Mr. Wenford? Or do you attend Miss Whyte at the Spragues?"

"No—that is, I thank you, but I am just on my way out." Wenfield raised both chin and eyebrows, as though his doings, which he had just made a point of revealing, were no concern of Hayden's.

"I do regret that, Mr. Wenton. Perhaps when I am at Ullswater, you will do me the honor."

"And that's another thing," Wenfield snapped. The man's disposition was truly most erratic. "What on earth do you do at Ullswater?"

"I visit, sir, and take the air."

"But you mentioned the Braughton properties. Why should they interest you?"

"They are very extensive properties, Wenleigh. They would be difficult to miss."

Wenfield frowned. "You mean that you are touring."

"That is one way of puttin' it, certainly."

"Well, I believe the Priory, at the old park just shy of Pooley Bridge, is usually open to view." Wenfield watched a servant serve out the soup. "But you should know that my parents do not in general welcome visitors at Hollen Hall, particularly this time of year."

"I am sorry to hear it. I understood the Duke of Braughton is known for his hospitality. Certainly he has always been most generous to me."

"To—you." As Hayden merely smiled and started on his broth, Wenfield asked, "By the by, who was that charming lady we saw you with last night? After the dance?"

Though he did not look up, Hayden caught Wenfield's "we."

"That," he said, making a point of taking another spoonful of soup, "was the Earl of Dalborough's daughter, Elissa Purvis." The claim was at least approximately true; Hayden hoped it would be even closer to truth by the following evening. For the moment, the description served, pricking Wenfield's pretensions. Hayden's thoughts moved on to Anne Whyte and her reference to "high company," which reference he now understood.

"I shall do you a favor, Myles," Wenfield offered grandly. "I shall mention your name at the Hall. Then, should you desire a visit, my parents might choose to receive you."

Hayden thanked him politely, held his laughter as the fellow strode importantly from the room, and finished his dinner with relish. By the time he stepped out later for his meeting with Anne Whyte, he so appreciated his own restored health and high spirits that he had no heart to consider their possible disappointment.

Chapter Seven

Her father made no further reference to the letter. Since Anne was used to hiding little from him, she found conversation on any other topic quite impossible. Thus, they parted for the evening with very few words between them and the letter safely snug in Mr. Whyte's coat pocket.

Anne had considered offering to take the gig on home with her father, but she knew she would only have had to return to town the following morning for church. More important, she had asked Mr. Myles to see her. Having arranged the appointment, she could not break it. That she had no wish to break it was something she scarcely admitted to herself.

She had dinner with the Spragues. After the meal, she sat sewing with Vera while Clement Sprague read aloud—a practice, he always claimed, that limbered his voice for the next morning's sermon. At the usual early hour, the couple bid her good night.

Anne claimed she would follow them up after she consulted some books in the vicar's library, a library that held among its treasures his late mother's volumes on gardening. As Anne often perused the titles, her preference went unremarked. Vera's maid, Price, and the housekeeper and the manservant retired to their own quarters before nine, leaving Anne in some mixed state of apprehension and anticipation, and very much alone.

She closed one of the half doors into the library, then peered outside from the side of the window drapes. Though it was only a quarter past nine, she wished to catch his arrival and keep him from waiting. In some agitation, she walked over to the hearth and turned down the wicks on the mantel's lanterns. She checked her reflection in the large, smoky mirror. To her mind, she looked worried, though she had changed before dinner and had made every effort to freshen her appearance as well as her spirits.

When she again looked out beyond the drapes, Mr. Myles stood outside by the tiny front gate, just steps from the stoop. Quickly, Anne moved to the front door and turned the key. The door opened soundlessly. Mr. Myles slipped into the dark vestibule. He smiled down at her as she closed the door behind him. With a nod to him, she led the way quietly into the library and shut the remaining half door.

"This is most inadvisable," he said softly as they moved together toward the hearth. But he smiled as he spoke, and the flickering light from the fire made him look like some summoned vision.

Shaking off the thought, Anne looked straight into those brilliant eyes.

"I assure you that it is no great risk to *you*. And for my part, if I did not trust you, I would not have asked you here."

Again the smile held her.

"Your frankness, Miss Whyte, is always refreshing."

He swiftly shed his greatcoat. At her gesture, they took seats on either side of the fireplace, though both leaned forward in order to speak low.

"You have walked far today?" he asked.

"I suppose I have." She shrugged. "I only realize it later."

He nodded but did not look pitying. Anne had known her limp was more pronounced, though she had attempted to hide it.

"I am pleased to see *you* looking so well, sir."

"I, too, have been walking." At her raised eyebrows, he added, "And resting."

She smiled. "I do not enforce prescriptions, sir. You mustn't be afraid of me."

"But I am afraid of you, Miss Whyte. Frightened quite beyond reason."

His serious tone, or his attention to her face, unnerved her. But Anne told herself that his intensity could indicate nothing too singular. The gentleman had courtly ways; she remembered his easy manners with another lady only the previous night.

"I cannot think why, Mr. Myles, since I have neither rank nor means."

"Ah! But that is the very reason I am afraid."

She did not understand him. But she hadn't time to inquire. The mantel clock chimed nine thirty, recalling her to the purpose of this rendezvous, one that *she* had requested.

"Should you like some port, sir?" She moved to stand, but he put out a hand to stop her. She nodded toward the cabinet behind his chair, and Mr. Myles rose to pour himself a half glass.

"You wish to keep me silent," he said lightly.

"I wish to keep you from coughing." She patted the small bundle of lozenges she had placed by her chair. "And this time I shan't forget to give you your lozenges."

"You are very prepared," he said, again taking a seat. "Are you certain *you* are not a spy, Miss Whyte?"

She blushed. "I do apologize for that. I was—quite upset—finding my father in those circumstances. I thought only of protecting him."

"I understood that at once. I understand it now. You must forgive *me*—for the reminder." He took a sip of the port. "You would, in fact, make a very poor spy, as you are much too pretty."

"Sir—"

"I did tell you this was inadvisable. I hope you had the foresight to dose the vicar's port."

Anne stifled a laugh. "This is all we need! To be discovered here late at night, laughing and sampling the port."

"There are worse things," he said, smiling.

"Yes—well." She breathed deeply. "I wished to discuss my father. You know him and have been treated to his views. Did you find what you heard at the pub this evening to be so very troubling?"

"Troubling, yes. As I told you, he thinks with his heart. And he is a man of strong, independent opinions. Have you seen him since?" At Anne's nod he asked, "And did he explain anything of his mission?"

"He said he was called to write a petition of complaint for

them, and that he did sign it as well. He suggested he has struck for English liberty."

Myles made some small sigh of frustration. "I do not know the other men," he said. "Who were they?"

"All are farmers from the area. Jamie—James—Ballard, concerns me most. He has a most belligerent nature, a quick anger. And a reputation for fighting. He farms just beyond Wiswood, toward the ferry. I believe he has had a difficult time with his leases. His two younger brothers have gone north to work at the mines. We have become quite industrial here, sir, despite the pretty fields in the vale."

He nodded in agreement.

"You will not recall it," she added, "but 'twas Mr. Ballard who brought you to me, in his wagon last week. I am certain someone here in town must have tipped him to bring you out—perhaps your Mr. Dilly—because Jamie Ballard would never have volunteered. He is that sort."

"He smells of strong beer and poultry yards, Miss Whyte. I remember *that* much."

"I hope it did not make you even more ill," she said, smiling at him.

"If so, he could have taken me no place better." He smiled back.

"And then"—she quickly swallowed—"there was Mr. Shanks, who is a landholder with a farm over Coniston way. One of his sons, William, went to Lancaster to find work. He was caught for breaking machines two years ago. Billy Shanks was transported." At this, she thought her guest looked rather severe. She hurried on. "Po Cowell is a tenant farmer on the Yardley estate just north of here. You can see the ancient pele tower—the new manor abuts it—from the road north to Ambleside."

"Yes," he said. "I have seen it."

"Why, when could you have been up there?"

"Yesterday. Do go on, Miss Whyte."

"Mr. Cowell is often in his cups, but then, in all fairness, I usually see him in town at the weekend. He has been troubled by illness in his family. He has eight children. But he has always been most kind to me." She raised her chin.

"And the one called Digweed?"

"I was surprised to see Mr. Digweed there, almost as surprised as I was to see Father. Thaddeus Digweed has a farm right here outside of Hawkshead. I had thought him prosperous, but I recall my father mentioning that he'd had to borrow to pay taxes. He must have other encumbrances—mortgages, perhaps. Many of the farmers about, though independent, are not quite freeholders. Their claims to the land are customary. I helped Mr. Digweed's wife some time ago. She passed on last year. I should have thought Mr. Digweed very steady." Speaking of Catherine Digweed saddened her; the woman had possessed a sweet nature, and suffered a most painful passing.

"You said that two of these men are tenant farmers. On whose land?"

"I believe Lord Tinsdale's."

Unexpectedly, he looked amused. "The Earl of Tinsdale?"

"Yes, I believe so."

He thought for a moment, idly thumbing the crystal of his glass of port.

"As you said," he sighed, "these are not *bad* men." She could not read his gaze in the firelight. "Except for Billy Shanks, who did break the law, as well as property. His father cannot be held to account. Heaven forbid that *I* should burden a father with the sins of a son." Some secret amusement graced his lips. "Transportation is harsh; punishments these days are excessive, perhaps because the stakes are so high. The revolution in France gave us a generation of war. No one wants revolution here."

"Grave matters indeed, sir, but I doubt these men incite revolt. They are English, after all."

Again she noted that small smile.

"They have legitimate grievances. But the manner in which they set about resolving them matters greatly. Harsh or threatening words will not serve them well. Why your father must feel obliged to sign a letter he merely composes on behalf of others—"

"He would always take responsibility for his own words." Anne spoke with pride—and an equal part of resignation.

"Certainly," he conceded, tilting his head, "a man must be permitted to write a letter in this country. And your father is, I grant you, a remarkable wordsmith." At her questioning look he explained, "I have been reading his first volume."

"I see."

"Is there a chance that this is not the only letter he has written? That perhaps, during his travels in the area, he has penned others?"

"Such never occurred to me." She clasped her hands tightly in her lap. "If so, 'twould be more serious, would it not? Might he be accused of sedition?"

He shook his head.

"Even had he written dozens, the situation is not that dire. A complaint is not a threat. And it is understandable that, in trying circumstances, these men should find solace in company. 'Twould be impossible for the authorities, however eager to promote stability, to prevent grumblings in pubs."

"But why should these men go so far as to *identify* themselves, to send a letter? Why not simply talk and . . . and merely share some ale?"

Again he sighed. "I have noticed before, at many levels, an ill-considered tendency to action, when time and patience alone might resolve many a problem. *Doing* something may ease an itch but often results in more harm than good."

Anne suggested ruefully, "My father would differ with you."

"So he does. He is an idealist. And perhaps he is right." Mr. Myles met her gaze. "But he worries his daughter. I would ask you not to worry."

"And this is all you advise me, then? Not to worry?"

"Would you have preferred I had not come?"

As she could not answer that honestly, she stayed silent. He watched her for a moment. The circumstances were decidedly intimate, here by the fireside, leaning toward each other. She might have touched his hands, had she reached for them. She found comfort merely in his presence.

"I am unfair," he said, setting his port aside. "When a lady presents a gentleman with a problem, that gentleman thinks he must attempt to solve it, whether or not the lady desires solutions. Sometimes the lady wishes only to express her unease, or fury, or both."

"Perhaps such *expression* is all that those who are powerless might effect."

He smiled. "Just so. But to prove that *you* are not powerless, Miss Whyte, I beg your forbearance to consider a few recommendations. The first would be that you seek the advice of your host, good Vicar Sprague. As a town resident, and a clergyman, he must know all the principals. Perhaps he will have some insights. Perhaps he might be prevailed upon to seek the confidence of your father, or one of the others, and either communicate the result to you or reassure you."

Anne nodded. "'Twas not my first impulse, but 'tis a good one."

"Or, you might approach one of the men yourself. You hesitate, understandably, to quiz your father for more. But you say you know Mr. Digweed, that you nursed his wife. Approached by you, in a confidential manner, he might reveal much."

Anne frowned at that possibility. "He might think me prying."

He shook his head, as though disputing that she could ever be thought prying, then offered, "My last suggestion—and probably the least acceptable to you—though I confess 'twas the first thought of *mine*—would be to intercept the letter."

"I did think of it. But I would never interfere with my father's correspondence."

"I suspected you would share your father's scruples."

"Which you appear to scorn."

"No. But as a practical matter, they are certainly inconvenient." He held her gaze. She thought his own a challenge. And she wondered if he spoke only of the letter.

"I suppose I might look for it tomorrow at home, though I believe he would have posted the letter this evening in town. He does make copies. He *might* have made a copy . . ."

"Should the copy be found, you might assure yourself of its import. Knowing *that* might preclude the need for anything else. And you would then think my simple suggestions annoying."

She blushed. "Since I sought your advice, I can hardly think them annoying, sir. Indeed, should I find a copy of the letter, I would ask, how might I let you know its contents?"

"Should you still wish to let me know, Miss Whyte?" His

gaze was very clear and direct. Again she could not answer him. If her father's words were indeed incriminating or embarrassing, she might not be eager to relay as much.

He leaned forward, his finely kept, pale fingers interlaced beyond his spotless cuffs. The only other estate agents she had met had spent considerable time on the properties they oversaw, and though they did not work the fields themselves, they were out among the landsmen, traveling in the sun and wind . . .

"He might be entirely innocent of all we imagine," he said.

"But you said you consider this serious."

"I do consider it serious. In fact"—he inched closer—"should you desire me to stay, Miss Whyte, to intercede, to press your father, or Mr. Digweed—"

Anne shook her head.

"I cannot ask it of you. It is gallant of you, sir. And you have been most generous with your time and advice."

"Which you will now ignore."

"I shall do nothing of the kind! I mean to—"

A sound from upstairs, a soft thud, instantly silenced her. She stared at the gentleman across from her, whose gaze had narrowed. He rose and walked quickly across to the library's door. Opening one panel, he looked into the center hall and up the stairs. When the sound failed to repeat, he returned to his chair but stood beside it at the hearth instead of resuming his seat. So positioned, he looked tall and imposing, and colder.

"You go tomorrow, then," she asked, remembering to keep her voice low, "to Ullswater?"

"Yes. Though I believe I must stop in Penrith first." His brow furrowed. Anne assumed something troubled him in his work.

"You know that Mr. Wenfield—that his parents lease Hollen Hall, one of the Braughton properties?" she asked.

"I have not forgotten."

"And do you make this visit because of the same sort of grievances, of laborers or tenants, that we heard this evening?"

As he smiled, his brow cleared.

"What a pertinent question, Miss Whyte. In fact, what draws my attention is the absence of such, apart from one letter. And yes"—he answered her unspoken question—"I mean to inquire as to its signatories. Otherwise, there has been nothing untoward, no news of upsets or reprimands. All is remarkably quiet. Most unusual, given the times."

She examined his face, which still looked pale.

"I burden you, sir, when you have concerns of your own. You anticipate some problems?"

He nodded sharply. "Your father no doubt shares the nature of estate difficulties with you. Any property has such. When there are none—well, I told you that I gamble. Such would be more than luck."

"And how long shall you stay?"

"I cannot say. Its duration has naught to do with my inclinations."

"I hope that your malady does not revisit you on this journey."

"I do not expect it to do so. It is too soon."

"But your fever has proved intermittent." She considered him closely. "I have never asked you to explain its origin. At dinner with my father, you mentioned the accident—"

"Do you ask as my doctor?" he asked lightly. When she faced him unperturbed, willing him to be serious, he shrugged. " 'Tis rather a dark memory."

"Then by no means—"

"Not at all. I find I wish to tell you." His fingers smoothed the high chair back before him. "I was sixteen, and swimming at the river, with my brother, David, and cousin Chas. We were used to diving and slipping through the lower gate of a weir. We'd done it hundreds of times, not only that summer but every summer before. So you understand, the task—the play—was quite routine. Nothing at the weir ever changed. But that afternoon, a metal hinge strap rusted out. The lower plank on the sluice gate fell just as David swept through. The plank secured him below." He tapped the back of the chair, then looked away from her and moved closer to the hearth.

"I had surfaced, expecting David behind me. When he didn't appear, I turned back at once. The plank had caught him at the ankle, trapping him at the bottom. The pressure of the current doubled the effect. 'Twas impossible for me to lift the plank. And after a few seconds, David ceased even to attempt to aid me."

Anne held her breath, even as she knew the gentleman before her recalled holding his.

"I had sense enough to break the plank, using the power of the river itself to kick at the wood. When it broke, the rush whisked me downstream but lifted David. Chas grasped him from above. I reached the shore at last; we hauled David to the bank. We held him upside down between us and shook him as vigorously as we were able. His color returned. He started to cough."

As though the memory alone might renew his cough, Mr. Myles touched a palm to his chest. "I felt the burn in my lungs then; I had been under a long while. I thought little of it at the time. But now"—his gaze met hers—"I am compelled to."

"You saved his life."

"I have not regretted it." The warmth of his smile made her blink. That she should be so besotted appalled her.

"You . . . you must be certain to rest. I should not keep you late again tonight." She watched his eyes and ventured to observe, "All of us stayed at our revelry much too late last night."

"Did you? I retired early."

"How can you say so! We saw you—" She stopped, worrying her lower lip, and looked to the fire. She had not meant to reveal so much. *An ill-advised meeting, indeed!*

"Clearly," he drawled after a second's silence, "there is too little to do here, that one's activities should be so scrutinized."

His superior tone had her straightening.

"'Tis impossible to miss four huge, spirited horses. And for a single lady's coach! I did not know you had acquaintance here in town."

"Nor did I."

He fenced with her. She frowned and rose from her chair.

"I thank you again for your time here tonight, sir. And for your confidences. But I will not keep you."

Something flashed in his blue gaze, something assessing or amused, or both. Anne tilted her chin and placed a hand upon the mantel for support.

"Miss Whyte dismisses me, then," he said, "because I have served my purpose? Or because my dissolute ways shock her saintly soul?"

"I am no saint—"

"Oh, no indeed! I had forgotten the way you permit every man in town to toss you about in the dance. And to think *waltzing* is considered risqué! No doubt you flirt with the populace as well."

Her hand on the mantel closed into a fist. "I do not flirt."

"You would hardly be the one to determine it."

"And you, sir, would be most unlikely to recognize a saint."

At the look on his face, she feared he would forget himself and laugh. Instead he reached quickly for her fisted hand and, opening her fingers within his own, moved to kiss her open, gloveless palm. His lips felt hot.

"You are splendid, Miss Whyte," he said softly, retaining her hand. "You would never marry Perry Wenfield."

He spoke as though he thought aloud. Anne found the compliment most curious. He paid tribute to her character, to her value, yet in asserting that she would reject another, *he* did not claim her. She decided he observed her, and others, as quite remote from himself. Though he held her hand, though his kiss had made her tremble, his detachment chilled her.

She drew her hand from his.

"You praise me for my frankness, Mr. Myles. But I fear I have been too candid regarding my circumstances. I should not have told you of Mr. Wenfield's offer. 'Twas imprudent of me, and discourteous to him. I hope I might rely on your honor, not to betray my trust."

"I would never betray your confidences, Miss Whyte. But I shall have no qualms about exposing *his* ambitions."

"Why should you wish to?"

He paused in the act of donning his coat. Watching him prepare to leave made Anne feel empty, nearly ill.

"There are several reasons, none of which I might relay to you. But one—and perhaps the most important—is that I am tempted to do so because he dares aspire to what I cannot."

"I had thought better of you, sir."

He looked perplexed. "I suspect we speak at cross purposes, Miss Whyte."

"I am sorry to hear it." She drew a deep breath and tried to smile. "During your stay with us I had thought we understood each other."

"I believe we do," he said lightly, but something grave in his expression belied any jest. As she became aware of simply standing and staring, he said, "It is late—"

"Yes—oh!" She stepped back to retrieve the small package of lozenges. She had rarely before been as conscious of her limp. "I should have been remiss had I again forgotten these." When she turned to hand the bundle to him, he again captured her bare hand.

"You have taken exceptional care of me, Miss Whyte. Be assured I shall do whatever I might to see that your father comes to no harm."

As her throat threatened to close upon her, she could do little more than nod.

He slipped her parcel into a pocket of his coat, then pressed her hand between both his palms. "Thank you. I hope that someday I might be able to make amends."

She thought he must mean to make up for her time and effort during his illness.

"There are no amends to be made."

"There most certainly are—or will be." His gaze was steady, but his meaning eluded her. When he quickly saluted her hand, she felt her face warm.

She saw him into the front hall. In the nighttime stillness, the hall clock's ticking sounded loud.

"Farewell, sir," she managed.

"Farewell—Anne," he whispered pointedly, and with one swift, intent glance, he let himself out.

Chapter Eight

I gather, my lord," Mr. Munroe said, "that you shall prosecute."

"No." Hayden turned from the window and the gray, rainy view of Penrith. "I shall not." At Munroe's surprise he added, "I have my reasons for declining to do so. His Grace would concur. You are certain of the accusations?"

"I await confirmations from town. But the local people I consulted on receiving your letter have all indicated the same. You might wish to wait for word from the City—should you prefer to confront the man only when all is definite. But if you do not plan to go to the law—"

"I think I might make clear to him my preferences even without such confirmations. He must leave Hollen Hall—that is a certainty."

"Why should you choose not to prosecute, though, my lord? Mr. Wenfield has stolen thousands from you, or I should say, from His Grace, from Braughton."

"Not from Braughton, Mr. Munroe. Those harmed in this instance are the tenants, who surrendered more in rents than they need have. Wenfield and the steward, Greeley, played a most reprehensible trick on them, as well as on us. Their crime was extortion more than theft. The farmers are due restitution. If Wenfield hasn't the funds—and I suspect he hasn't—then Braughton must and will restore the monies."

"But, my lord! With a rent roll here of ten thousand, 'twill eliminate five years of income from the properties!"

" 'Tis an excessive amount, I know. But there are other properties. Braughton will not long suffer from the lack. And trust must be regained. We might only do that by ridding the tenants of Wenfield and returning what is rightfully theirs."

From over his spectacles, Mr. Munroe peered at him.

"'Tis an unusual course, Lord Hayden. What of Wenfield? He cannot stay in the area. And he will have little on which to live."

"We shall let him keep enough to ship his family and all belongings to America or the West Indies—or even farther, if he chooses. Perhaps he still has energy to apply himself to accumulating another fortune. His own, of course." His quick smile was grim. "He succeeded once. Whatever led him to risk so much, whether a failure of judgment or a pressing need, we might never know. Perhaps I shall discover it. In any event, he shall have had a chance to learn, and another to redeem himself. Those he has injured will never be as fortunate."

"What of the son, my lord?"

"Mr. Perry Wenfield"—Hayden's gaze returned to the bleak streets outside—"must do as he chooses. He might fail here as easily as elsewhere." Catching himself at sounding spiteful, he added, "We've had no indication that he knew of his father's scheme. 'Tis possible he had no knowledge of it. I believe he's spent much of his time away, at university or traveling. If he did participate in this fraud, however, the same punishment should apply—to restore what was taken, and then move on."

His concern, of course, was Anne Whyte. He had told her so emphatically that she would never marry Perry. He had said so with the confidence—the arrogance—that only *he* deserved her. But if young Mr. Wenfield's family and fortune were ruined, then, yes, she might be so foolish as to sacrifice herself. She was that sort.

He started to cough. He had not coughed at all in days. As he reached for one of the lozenges in his waistcoat pocket, he turned to a concerned-looking Mr. Munroe and shook his head.

"'Tis the weather," Hayden said when he could speak, the lozenge safely lodged atop his tongue. *Horehound again,* he thought, and some elusive flavor that reminded him strongly of Anne Whyte's garden. He did not believe he suffered from the weather; he blamed his decline on frustration and an accompanying ill temper. He despaired at the prospect of living with either.

Mr. Munroe was shaking his head. "I cannot understand it! For Mr. Wenfield to attempt to make up his losses in such a manner!"

"Yes. 'Tis unconscionable, but 'tis not too late. How Wenfield planned to settle and reside in the area after this, I cannot fathom. His persistence speaks of immeasurable gall. A mark, I warrant, of those who engage in such swindles."

"Had you not come north, my lord," Munroe said, "I should never have looked for discrepancies. I believed any complaints about high rents and taxes merely to be part of the general discontent."

"There is certainly enough of that, Mr. Munroe." Hayden again turned from the window, this time walking back toward the agent's wide mahogany desk. "You mustn't fault yourself, sir." He was rewarded with a grateful nod of the head. "An unusual circumstance placed me in a position to hear some of the grumbling and charges against Braughton. That is the major reason I had suspicions."

"'Twas foolish to air such in your hearing, my lord."

Hayden merely smiled. "With the war and its prosperity for the countryside, such excesses were hidden. But given this year's collapse and the imposition of the Corn Laws, the pinch has been severe. Mr. Wenfield knew he could not continue. 'Tis why he sought to leave Hollen and build elsewhere. But his luck was out." Hayden paced with the restlessness that had beset him the past few days. "I have sent a note to my father. He will anticipate one from you as well. And, though I think it unlikely, we should alert all Braughton's agents to look for similar disparities at other properties." He paused. "'Tis ironic, that Father encourages keeping the rents low for those he likes—but he has never liked Wenfield." Hayden's lips rose as he met Munroe's gaze. "This has been unfortunate from start to finish."

Munroe concurred. He ordered in some refreshments. Then he turned to instructing a clerk in copying those items Lord Hayden wished to take away with him.

Hayden sipped the welcome hot coffee. On arriving in Penrith Sunday evening, two days ago, he had sought out Munroe. In perusing the agent's accounts, he had once again been struck by the absence of any difficulties or late payments from the Hollen

Hall property, though the income had fallen off. Hayden had asked Munroe to send a man out to inquire of the farmers just how they fared, what they were paying in rent and how frequently—an inquiry that had revealed an unexpected and enormous disparity between what Wenfield had demanded and collected, and what had been sent on to Munroe. The farmers had been forwarding, on extortionary terms, almost twice the usual rents to Wenfield, who had apparently been attempting to restore the fortune he had lost on an ill-judged canal investment. Munroe awaited further word from his contacts in the City regarding the extent of that investment loss. But Wenfield's motive in resorting to dishonesty and theft did not really matter; the effect had been unforgivable.

Hayden controlled his fury that Wenfield had let the Duke of Braughton be blamed for maladministration and greed. But Hayden chose to be more generous than his inclinations directed. It would never have been the gentlemanly course to ruin the father of a rival. And Hayden could not think of Perry Wenfield as anything but a rival.

"You will be traveling to the Priory this evening, my lord?" Munroe asked.

"Yes, and on to Hollen tomorrow. I should like this resolved quickly, within a couple of days at most. I wish to return to Leicestershire before the snow flies."

"Certainly the roads will be better. And I know there is fair hunting to be had in that county before the frost."

"'Tis well known that you are fond of the sport, Mr. Munroe. I tend to prefer the shooting. But no, I return because of my father's letter. The letter you held for me, sir. My *grand-mère*— the dowager duchess—is ailing."

"I am sorry to hear it. I had the privilege of meeting your grandmother once, many years ago. Her Grace was most enchanting."

Hayden nodded. His *grand-mère* did indeed have a reputation for being "most enchanting." But having received much in the way of scolding from her over the past dozen years, Hayden knew another side of his charming relative. What she would make of his latest predicament he could well guess.

"Indeed," he agreed. "She is a magnificent lady. I am exceedingly fond of her. But she has entered her ninth decade, and cannot always advance in step with her high spirits."

Mr. Munroe acknowledged the truth of that with a slight nod. Abruptly, Hayden paced once more.

"There is another matter," he said. "I made the acquaintance in Hawkshead of a Mr. Whyte. Everett Whyte, with a *y*. He has been traveling in the Lakes, researching a history. Unfortunately, he has supplemented that undertaking by serving as composer and scribe, in writing to various landowners on behalf of aggrieved tenants. I wonder if you recall having seen his name on any correspondence regarding Braughton properties? Perhaps even on that one letter that drew my father's interest?" He hoped rather than expected that Munroe would deny any knowledge of Anne Whyte's father.

Munroe's wild brows lowered as he mulled over the name.

"Everett Whyte. E. Whyte. That does sound familiar. Though with regard to anything relating to Braughton, of course . . ."

Hayden found the pause unbearable. "Perhaps if I might simply review some of this past year's correspondence?" he suggested. "While I await the Wenfield documents?"

"Certainly, my lord. Though you know we send summaries of all incidental correspondence to His Grace."

"Yes, I am aware of it, sir. You had summarized that one letter. But you quite rightly do not list every signatory of such a missive. 'Twould be pointless replication. I thought I might check."

Munroe rang for the year's correspondence to be brought to Hayden. A clerk soon appeared with three flat boxes.

"Might I help you, Lord Hayden?" Munroe asked, and Hayden agreed with a nod. There was nothing the agent might see that he had not already seen.

"What of Greeley, my lord—the steward at Hollen?" Munroe asked. They had spread the letters out on a table before the window. "You would not prosecute him and let Wenfield fly?"

"No. We shall turn Greeley out sans reference. I feel obliged to protect others from the services of such a serpent of a steward. His savings also must be seized, of course. I assume I shall see Greeley when I meet Wenfield at the Hall."

"My lord, perhaps you might wish—" He cleared his throat. "I hesitate to suggest it, Lord Hayden, but perhaps you will consent to take some protection along with you?"

"You expect me to be attacked, Mr. Munroe?"

"Such is likely, my lord. As the bearer of bad news—"

"I should think the added risk to them hardly worth the undoubted pleasure of thrashing me."

"These will be desperate men, Lord Hayden!"

"But they will not know themselves desperate until I have opened my mouth. And the first thing I shall say is that I will not bring charges. *That* will astonish them. No, Mr. Munroe. I believe I might travel west without an entourage. You might, indeed, even safely accompany me."

"I would be most honored to accompany you, my lord."

But Hayden, who had been teasing, convinced Mr. Munroe to stay in Penrith, as insurance against the unlikely event that something untoward should indeed take place. They did agree to send two riders immediately to watch the roads from Hollen pending Hayden's arrival, in the event that Greeley or Wenfield should attempt to abscond.

In silence, then, they quickly searched through the correspondence, looking only for the signature *Whyte*. At the bottom of the second box, Hayden found it on an August letter—a very brief letter, but elegantly worded for all that. In reading the missive through a second time, Hayden wished he had the same gift for language.

The letter's import was reassuringly far from threatening. The signatories "begged leave to bring to the attention of His Grace" various difficulties encountered in meeting payments, though the payments had, of course, been met. The action requested of the Duke of Braughton was mere consideration, not quite a demand for redress. The letter listed another man in Penrith as a contact for further information. But the signature at the very bottom was definitely that of the author: *E. Whyte*.

As Myles pocketed the page, he calculated how quickly he might convey to Anne Whyte the relatively tame tone of her father's communication. Then he wondered if he could rightly do so. He had access to this letter to Braughton but not to any sent elsewhere. And all might not have had as mild an import.

While awaiting the papers from Munroe's clerk, Hayden penned brief letters to those landowners he knew and believed most likely to have received a letter from Whyte. Then, in possession of the evidence of Wenfield's manipulations, Hayden departed.

He stayed at the Priory, which, despite its name, had probably never been used as one. The ruins of a Norman church had provided footings for an eighteenth-century improvement—the nave converted to a central hall, and the apparent cloistral foundations becoming bases for two comfortable wings of rooms. The house was not the largest or most imposing. But set at lakeside, in the middle reach of Ullswater and upon one of its gentler shores, it boasted a splendid view of both the water and the enclosing heights.

Hayden had not returned even once since age thirteen; nonetheless, he was fond of the spot: the trees, the lake, the dramatic fells. His servants had enjoyed a holiday while he had recuperated in Hawkshead; their looks that evening when he returned from Penrith were sheepish. Perkins, upon Hayden's inquiry, advised him of his last sighting of the eloping Henry Purvis and Miss Birdwistle.

"I helped see 'em off in a chaise and four at Carlisle, my lord."

"Well done, Perkins. And the bays?"

"Would ha' run clear to the border, if'n I'd asked it, milord. Only you said to spare 'em, and the chaise was ready to be had. The bays were right eager for the journey, I can tell you."

"I shall take them to Hollen Hall tomorrow morning, Perkins. 'Tis only a short distance, but I should like to drive again." Once more, he envisaged Anne Whyte's slender, capable hands upon her mare's reins. No minute seemed to pass without some similar, unsought thought of her. His attachment, Myles thought, held the quality of an illness of its own.

Had he been able to indulge only in thoughts of *her,* the matter might have been resolved, one way or another. But the business with Wenfield had gone on long enough. And then Grand-mère!

At the moment, he might only relieve Anne Whyte of some of the concern for her father.

He ate a solitary, contemplative dinner, debating with himself how best to approach Wenfield. Yet there was only so much he could plan, as he did not know the man or his steward, or whether Wenfield's precious son would be in attendance.

The next morning, he and Perkins took the bays for their outing. Hayden felt the strength in his arms with satisfaction; the fever had left him weak for too many days. That feeling of strength increased his confidence; he knew he would again hone his body. But he was less sanguine about disciplining his thoughts. And the restoration of his peace of mind appeared very much a gamble, one left entirely to Anne Whyte. He worried again that she might never forgive.

The Hall, which qualified as both picturesque and imposing, with its extensive formal gardens amid the shadow of the crags, stood less than thirty minutes' drive from the Priory. The Elizabethan builders had constructed Hollen around an older, central pele tower, which remained only as a relic. The Hall, both older than the Priory and much roomier, oversaw the Duke of Braughton's largest estate in Cumberland. Hayden understood the attraction of the place for a man like Wenfield, who had needed, and sought, affirmation of his standing.

He drew the team to a halt in front of the house. Perkins jumped down to take the horses' heads before the Hollen groom could approach them. Hayden met Perry Wenfield's astonished gaze, because the young man stood gaping in the Hall's portico.

"That team," he gasped, as Hayden also leaped down to the ground. "I saw them in Hawkshead! Friday—"

"Most likely," Hayden said shortly.

"But why have you got 'em? They cannot be *jobbers!*"

"Thank you. Of course they are not. They are mine."

"*Yours?*"

"May I come in, Mr. Wenfield?" Hayden had reached the step just below Perry, which meant his gaze was only a couple of inches below the younger Wenfield's. Perry, though puzzled, no longer sneered.

"Well, yes. I guess so. Father knows of you—"

He shall shortly know much more, Hayden thought grimly as he mounted the final step and strode on into the house. He released his coat to a hovering butler, then lifted a brow impatiently at Perry, who appeared to be appraising Hayden's wardrobe.

"If you will, come through. I just left my parents in the drawing room."

They had scarcely made it through the door to the drawing room when Wenfield senior turned from a window looking out upon the road.

"Who was—" Wenfield stopped. His ruddy face instantly whitened, turning almost the color of his hair. *"Hayden!"*

"You remember me, Mr. Wenfield. It has been some years." Wenfield had not saluted him. Hayden turned to Mrs. Wenfield, who watched her husband's face with alarm. With a deep bow, he acknowledged, "Mrs. Wenfield."

She managed a curtsy, but her lips were trembling. The lady of the house was on the point of tears. Hayden considered it for the best when she left the room. Obviously she knew something of her husband's dishonest dealings. In glancing toward Perry, Hayden was less certain of the son.

"What is all this, Father? You call him 'Hayden,' but his name is Myles. I told you I'd met him."

"Lord Hayden," Wenfield said at last, though he still dispensed with the courtesy of a bow. "Apparently you have already met my son. Perry, this is the Marquis of Hayden."

"Marquis? You mean Braughton's—?"

"I am the Duke of Braughton's eldest son, yes." Perry, unlike his father, was turning bright red, as though he meant to dispute the relationship. "Would you mind, sir, if I had a few minutes alone with your father?"

"Mind? Look here—"

"Perry." His father's voice was weary but stern. "Please see to your mother."

With ill grace, Perry turned on his heel and, quitting the room, slammed the door.

"Do forgive him, my lord. He was taken by surprise."

Hayden tilted his head. He thought it unlikely he would ever forgive Perry Wenfield much of anything. But there were larger matters afoot.

"Mr. Wenfield, you must know why I have come."

Wenfield appeared to lose what little color he had regained. In his youth, he must have been a good-looking man—not, Hayden realized sourly, unlike his son. He retained fine features and an athletic, though heavy, build. But his expression was not one Hayden could admire. Wenfield's gaze had narrowed, and that gaze held too much calculation.

"I am afraid I do not—"

"The rents, sir." Hayden drew the slim oilskin pouch from beneath his arm and started to untie it. "There have been discrepancies."

"Surely not? I have always sent on to Mr. Munroe everything owing."

"But you have also taken more than was owed." Hayden held Wenfield's attention. "I do not wish to belabor the point. Is Mr. Greeley about?"

Wenfield nodded and, signaling the footman, directed him to find the steward. Once the servant had left, he said, "I am certain we must be able to sort this out."

"I, also, am certain of it. In fact, I have sorted it out."

Wenfield's nostrils flared. He was unused to being ordered.

"If you are so certain, my lord, why do you not bring a magistrate?"

"Because, Mr. Wenfield, if you and Mr. Greeley will meet my conditions, I do not intend to prosecute."

Wenfield's expression eased.

"You have no proof," he said, with obvious satisfaction.

"On the contrary. You would be most unwise to think so." Hayden turned at the sound of the door. A man he took to be Greeley, the steward, stood there with a hand inside his coat. Undoubtedly he had a pistol or a knife. "I know you are a most enterprising sort, Mr. Greeley," Hayden said, "and used to enforcing much. But you would be ill-advised even to think what you are thinking. I have just been explaining to Mr. Wenfield why the law does not accompany me."

Greeley glanced to Wenfield, then removed his hand from his coat. Unlike the members of the family, he did not turn color or weep. Hayden gauged that, with that frozen a countenance, the man might callously kill someone. He wondered who had trusted his face enough to hire him. If the mild-mannered Mr. Munroe were responsible, Hayden must suggest he correct his spectacles.

"What do you propose, Lord Hayden?" Wenfield asked.

"That you restore the difference in the rents and quit Hollen. That Mr. Greeley do the same. Mr. Munroe has helpfully supplied a bill." Hayden handed the sheet to Wenfield, who glanced at it with a stony expression.

"I am surprised, my lord, that you would come here today on such an errand." Greeley's accents were gravelly, very north country, and decidedly aggressive. He was a large man, and one clearly used to intimidating.

"Would you rather I had sent the bailiffs, Greeley?"

Wenfield handed the sheet to the steward.

"I shall have to sell some shares," Wenfield said heavily, "and consols, and some of our personal belongings . . ."

Hayden stood without commenting. How the man extricated himself at this point did not interest him. But Wenfield had seen the bill; honor demanded that he pay it.

"After this, I'll never work again," Greeley said condemningly, waving the bill.

"Surely that was your wish, Mr. Greeley—to have engaged in this venture at all. I fear I cannot supply a character."

Greeley's dour face darkened.

"How long?" Wenfield asked dully.

"The monies returned within a fortnight and your removal within the same. I'll ask both of you to sign that bill. You must work out between you whatever proportion suits. You will be held accountable in any event, one for the other."

"I might still be short," Wenfield said.

Hayden had no sympathy for the man. For years Wenfield had lived well while those under his care had gone without.

"You may choose to leave the country. In fact, I would encourage it. I cannot preserve your reputation."

"I'll not sign anything," Greeley asserted coldly. "If you'd had proof, you'd have brought a magistrate." Abruptly he turned to go.

"'Tis a pity you scorn this chance when offered to you, Greeley," Hayden said. "You are a thief. If you leave the room without signing the bill, you will most assuredly be pursued and charged. Mr. Wenfield may carry the debt, but you shall be the one in prison."

Greeley hesitated only a moment. He sent Hayden a venomous look, then walked out without sparing a glance at his former partner.

"If you take him to law, you must also take me," Wenfield said.

"Not if you sign the bill, even if you cannot pay it all at once. Mr. Greeley is a fool."

"I was a fool for listening to him." Wenfield sighed and looked at him very directly. "Lord Hayden, my son knows nothing of this."

"I am glad to hear it."

"My wife and I will probably remove to Barbados, where she has family. But Perry—Perry might wish to stay. He has been courting—" Wenfield paused, then abruptly leaned to his desk, to grab his quill pen and sign the bill.

If you but knew, Hayden thought, watching him, *how Perry's "courting" has spared you!*

"I shan't need much longer than a week to arrange my departure," Wenfield said, "if Mr. Munroe would kindly handle the sale of some personal property. There is no value in delaying."

Hayden nodded to him. The man was decisive, a quality he respected. Apart from the one reference to Greeley's influence, there had been no effort at excuses.

"Should I write to your father—to His Grace?" Wenfield asked as though there were a standard for such a unique instance.

"He will not expect it."

Wenfield frowned. "Why do you trouble with this, Lord Hayden? Why did you not simply send Munroe and the law?"

Again Hayden had to credit Wenfield's acuity.

"I also have gambled and lost, Mr. Wenfield." And then, because he was curious, he asked, "Why did you risk so much?"

"It is the only way I know how to live."

Hayden understood him. Such a man, who had started with nothing, must always have felt there was little to preserve. Reward would only have been gained by extreme risk and, once he had accumulated much, accumulating more. He had trusted to his own golden touch. But his instincts had betrayed him.

Despite his distaste for the manner in which Wenfield had furthered his ambition, Hayden had to respect that he had taken failure well. The son, Hayden thought, was unlikely to perform as admirably.

The only way I know how to live. Hayden found himself silently repeating the comment. He could not help but think of Anne Whyte, and of her influence upon him. She deserved more from him, certainly—an explanation, at the least, and perhaps a less careful and cowardly preservation of his countenance. There would have been no harm in giving her an assurance of his regard.

He regretted his distance, as he had never regretted it before. Though he believed he had chosen the proper course in leaving her, he acknowledged that he had behaved most *im*properly for their entire acquaintance. His interests and desires, *Braughton's* interests and desires, had proved paramount. It had been, he thought, the way he had always lived. But the goal of redeeming himself now energized him.

He summoned Munroe out to the Priory for a discussion of next steps. The agent returned to Penrith with charges to the local magistrates regarding Greeley, who had been stopped within a mile of Hollen Hall. Early the following morning Hayden had his household harness the bays and pack two coaches. Then, despite the persistent urge to head south to Wiswood and return immediately to Anne Whyte, he directed his coachman home to Braughton.

Chapter Nine

Anne had looked for him in church that Sunday, though he had said he would not attend. She continued to look for him in every familiar venue, knowing that there was no probability he was to be found.

"I am quite certain he will return shortly," Vera told her. "I have never seen a man so smitten."

"I must tell the vicar that he does not look 'smitten' enough."

Vera laughed.

"Do not be dispirited, Anne. Why do you fret?"

"I think I had best put thoughts of Mr. Myles away, Vee. Though I believe his attentions were sincere, there was always something *distant* in his manner. And I remind myself that he was in my care. He was civil, and he was appreciative. That is all."

Vera looked askance.

"A man who is merely 'civil' does not look as he looked. He does not rise from his sickbed to dance only with you. From what you say, he must have been concerned about his work, yet he stayed. To oblige you, Anne."

"He may have stayed for another reason. I told you about the lady after the dance—the lady with the superior carriage horses."

"You are too quick to judge. Recall that Mr. Myles is a gentleman of the world; his address, his speech, his clothing, everything about him told you so! His acquaintance must be vast. What I think, dearest, is that you search for a reason to think ill of him."

Anne turned her face away and stared very hard at the shelves of preparations and potions in her herb closet. Nothing had been the same—not her home, not her work, not even her family and friends. *He* intruded.

Vera had come to visit that morning to obtain, as she claimed, something more to ease the discomfort Mr. Tate felt with his broken leg. Vera never needed a reason to come calling. Anne looked again to her friend, sitting in the chair by the fire, Elijah comfortably nestled in her lap. Anne had not told her about the last meeting with Mr. Myles; she was too conscious of its impropriety. The conference had been late, in her hosts' home, in secret and solitude. And now she could speak neither of her concern about her father nor of her ailing heart.

"You miss him," Vera said.

"Yes. But I believe this no different from times past, when I have had other people as patients. You recall when Mrs. Matheson stayed here ten days? I missed *her.*"

Vera pursed her lips and shook her head. "I wish I had your skills, Anne. I would concoct a potion to make you honest."

"I *am* honest! I told you I miss him."

Vera still shook her head. "I suppose you will tell me next that you seriously entertain young Mr. Wenfield's suit?"

"As I know him so little, Vee, 'tis impossible to entertain it seriously. I have never encouraged him. But I cannot entirely dismiss him. If I should wish to marry—to have children—I might do much worse than Perry Wenfield." Her gaze slid to her garden, through the closed glass doors. The day had been chilly. It was cozier here inside.

"But you might do so much better! Why do you speak this way now? You have never before sounded so resigned."

"'Tis not 'resigned' to be rational, to be wise."

"'Tis heartless."

Anne smiled. "Perhaps so."

"He said nothing to you, then?"

"Mr. Myles?"

Vera looked her impatience. "Since Perry Wenfield says much too much to you, of course I mean Mr. Myles."

"He said that he knew I would never marry Perry Wenfield."

"Ah! You see?" In slapping the arm of the rocking chair, Vera disturbed Elijah, who jumped off her lap and moved to the opposite side of the hearth.

"You mustn't misunderstand," Anne said. "I know he did not intend—he could not possibly have meant—that he would offer, or even that he believed me destined for anyone other than Perry Wenfield. He meant only to compliment me."

"And so he did, as any jealous man might."

"I see we come about in a circle." Again Anne attempted to concentrate on her measurements.

"You should have worked some potion on Mr. Myles," Vera suggested, "to keep him here."

"'Twould not have lasted. And he would have resented it."

Vera stared at her open-mouthed. "Do you mean to tell me— that you might have concocted such a potion?"

Anne smiled. "Not for someone of so strong a will. I tell you, Vee, he clearly had other obligations. I must respect him for his discipline, for fulfilling those obligations, for keeping his promises. He made none to me."

"He *looked* them."

"However much I might wish it, that is not enough. Now do try to sit quietly for a minute, Vee, as I shouldn't wish to poison Mr. Tate."

When Anne at last looked up from her work, Vera was observing her with consideration.

"I should like you to accompany me to Kendal tomorrow," Vera said. "To see my cousin Mrs. Pomfret. Flora would entertain us both for a couple of nights. She is prone to nervous disorders, or so she tells me. I thought you might see her."

"I should be happy to. Has she consulted a physician?"

"I haven't a clue. She writes with a concern, and of course I think of you. And I must also do some shopping."

"I see. Had you determined on the shopping before you received your cousin's letter?"

"Need you ask?" Vera laughed as she stood. She leaned to stroke Elijah and murmur apologies.

"I shall check with Father, but I doubt he will object."

"It does you good, Anne, to be away. Your father must manage without you. You manage without him far too frequently."

"He researches his history, Vee. And since I do not mind his absences, why should you?"

"I so hate to see you wasted!"

"*Wasted!* So that is what you think of me!"

"Oh, I do not mean to sound intemperate."

"You do. And in a vicar's wife, it is most inappropriate."

Again Vera laughed. "So it is. But what I mean to say, dearest, is that he should have taken you to London, or Bath, or even Harrogate, and let you frequent the theater and the museums and mingle with—oh, with those who would know how to *value* you. Those who also are clever and kind and accomplished and—"

"Eligible," Anne supplied, carefully sealing the cap to Mr. Tate's salve. "I have just met an impressively clever, accomplished, and eligible gentleman—'tis debatable just how *kind* he might be—and he will not have me. 'Twould seem that Father properly gauged my attractions and spared himself much inconvenience."

"Mr. Myles will return," Vera repeated and then, at Anne's raised eyebrows, added, "and if he does not, there are always others."

"I thought you meant to argue that Mr. Myles was exceptional."

Vera *tsked.*

"I am leaving you," she said with an emphatically raised chin, "and your distressing logic. No wonder you are glum, if this is the manner in which you discourse! You must amuse only yourself with such arguments." She accepted the jar of salve. "But I shall still plan to meet you at the crossroads beyond Wiswood early tomorrow. Seven?" When Anne nodded, Vera kissed her on the cheek. "Pray, do not win *all* your solitary debates, Anne. You must leave some room for hope."

Anne found her father at his desk in his library, surrounded by open books and stacks of notes. She mentioned Vera's visit and the proposed trip to Kendal, to which her parent lent enthusiastic endorsement.

"I cannot say that I will not miss you, my dear. But you see that I am busily employed. I shall stay out of mischief."

"Shall you, Papa?" Anne could not prevent her concerned tone. In a most cursory glance through the papers at hand in his library, she had not seen any copies of correspondence, and she refused to prowl through his cupboards and drawers. "Have you only been working on your history, then?"

"Why, what else do you imagine intrigues me so, Anne? A translation of Sanskrit?"

She smiled. "I thought, perhaps, some correspondence."

"There is always correspondence, my dear; 'tis the greatest bane in life for any man who would prefer to accomplish something. But I suspect you refer to particular correspondence— with gentlemen visitors, perchance?"

Anne blushed. "I would have told you if that were the case, sir. And it is not."

"Then I fear I do not comprehend."

"I thought you might have particular concerns regarding the farms and the tenants or workers. Vera said—" Anne swallowed with the lie. "Vera said there has been much muttering in town."

"There is. And oft times the most from those least affected. But no, our little establishment does well. And your father was just wise enough never to have mortgaged the place. None of us shall starve, though I must say"—he leaned back in his chair and frowned—"the household accounts have seen a most astonishing rise in expenses."

"'Tis the prices, Father. I cannot limit some costs."

"And should not. Of course the prices are deplorable. I tease you, my dear. You mustn't worry."

Advised once more not to worry!

"I do not ask for myself, sir, but because I am concerned—for men like Mr. Digweed . . ."

"Ah, Digweed." He tapped his fingers upon his desk. "Truly, Anne, I know you were fond of his wife. But as you are aware, Mr. Digweed's precious plot is heavily encumbered. He attempts to renegotiate the notes. And though he is a most respectable gentleman, he has made choices—choices *I* should not have made."

"Of what nature, Father?"

He peered at her. "He has purchased items he could not afford, on credit, thus gambling on continued prosperity. He continues to give that wastrel of a son an enormous allowance. But see here, I trust you to treat all this in confidence. Does it ease your mind, daughter, or give you the headache?"

She did not know how to answer him. He attempted to help their neighbors and others—of that she had no doubt. She wished she might be equally certain of his good judgment. So she pressed him.

"You have not promised him anything?"

Again her father's glance was keen.

"Not one penny to the man, I swear it. I confess, I haven't a clue"—and now he rose and moved around toward her—"what concerns you. What is it, my dear?"

"I overheard you, by chance, at the Blue Duck. On Saturday evening. With Mr. Digweed and the others. I had no notion you were there, Papa. I did not mean to listen. But Jamie Ballard— you know he always brings trouble!"

"Ah, yes, Ballard. Well." Anne noticed that her father's gaze left her as he firmed his lips. "All I have done for him, Anne, is pen that petition to Lord Tinsdale, acquainting him with some matters of which he may not be aware. All of the men there at the pub had the same complaint, but would have had to approach three different magistrates, and singly, to address it. And one of those magistrates, Sir Ogden Berry, is infirm. I simply wrote a letter for my fellows, my dear, as I told you. You must not upset yourself."

"But why must *you* do this? Why can they not write for themselves? They are none of them unschooled."

"Ah, you think me flattered into service! Would you have me deny my time, and those few skills I possess, to my neighbors? Shall I ask you, Anne, not to engage in the effort and expense you do to help those who seek you out?"

"No, Father." She glanced to the floor. "You are right."

"I cannot preach to you, Anne. You know I do not attend Mr. Sprague on a Sunday as often as I ought. But there are principles for free men everywhere. I must contribute wherever I can, even for someone like Ballard."

As Anne nodded, he raised her chin and kissed her on the cheek. "Go to Kendal," he said, pulling a guinea from his waistcoat pocket. "Spend this on something you do not need. And do not give another thought to Mr. Digweed, Ballard, your father—or any other man. We are not worthy of you, my dear."

Vera had a tendency to drive much too slowly. During the weeks she and her husband spent in Hawkshead, Vera not only filled her days seeing to those church tasks that required her time, but, more satisfactorily, gathering news to share with Anne. She had not come close to exhausting her trove of gossip the previous afternoon. Now the combination of an enervating pace and a surfeit of chatter lent Anne's thoughts too many opportunities to slip away.

". . . or so I told her. What do you think of that, Anne? *Anne?*"

"I'm sorry, Vee. I was not listening."

"I suspect you have not heard a word since we left the ferry! Really, Anne, are you certain you are not in love?"

Anne could not stop her blush. "Do let me have the ribbons," she said quickly. "The horse looks near to dropping from boredom."

"Clement would have me spare him."

"I am certain this animal gets enough sleep, Vee. And I should like to reach Kendal today."

"Oh, very well, if driving will keep you attentive! You do drift off in the most curious manner. And your gowns begin to hang on you. You are sickening for something, dearest, and I suspect it is Mr. Myles. I am tempted to write to him."

Anne pushed the horse into a trot.

"If you do so, I shall never speak to you again."

"I shouldn't care for *that,* of course. Particularly since I mean to ask you to be godmother."

Anne looked to her in astonishment. "Vee! How can you talk incessantly and still be so sly? Does Clement know?"

"I shall tell him on our return. I intend to select some items for our nursery while in Kendal, then present him with the inescapable fact."

Anne pulled to a halt long enough to embrace her friend.

"You certainly have my attention now." She laughed. "I am so, so happy for you both! You shall be the very best of parents."

The journey then passed swiftly, with discussion of names, schooling, possible companions, avocations, vocations, and the best qualities in a spouse.

"We shall have nothing left to talk over on the way back," Anne observed, "as the poor babe is now well into middle age."

"Hush," Vera said, pushing playfully at her arm. "On the return, we shall discuss *you*," which threat left Anne again silent.

They reached the Pomfrets' home, where Vera's elderly cousin Flora greeted them with relief and lamentations. She had too many pains to enumerate, she did not sleep, food left her ill, she felt too weak to take exercise, and every sound from the street deafened her. Mrs. Pomfret, Anne advised, suffered from a severe nervous disorder. Anne prepared her fresh-brewed pekoe and rose hip tea, in which she floated a decorative piece of candied angelica. After half an hour's discussion, Mrs. Pomfret, claiming that she felt much better, retired to her bedchamber to nap.

Once their hostess had left, Anne smiled at Vera.

"She will be much improved in the morning. All she wants is company and something to do. We must devise some task for her, Vee."

"You did not put any of your preparations into her tea?"

"Not one. Except for a small portion of sugar, of course."

"I did not think you capable of it."

"Of what?"

"So much deception."

"Tea is a tonic. And so, apparently, are we. Where is the deception in that?"

Vera shook her head.

"'Tis love that makes you so secretive, Anne. I wonder what else you keep from me?"

Anne again fell silent.

They went out for a walk along Highgate and down to the banks of the river. They knew they might claim perhaps only one more week of fair weather, as there had already been a frost at night. Despite Vera's news, despite the anticipation and prospect of months of preparation, Anne felt the grayness of her surroundings: the monotony of the limestone houses; the cold, streaming river; the heavy sky. She thought of her sister, Sarah, in childbed, and feared for Vera. She thought of Perry Wenfield and of marriage, and feared for herself. Once again she recalled her recent patient's fair head.

A night's rest had her waking determined to put thoughts of Mr. Myles aside. At breakfast she and Vera drew up a list of necessities for a nursery, which included the very finest mahogany cradle available, and a longer list of those items merely desired. Then they set out briskly, before the Pomfrets had even awakened, to fulfill both lists as requirements.

By midmorning they had reviewed and purchased enough items to supply several establishments of their own. At the draper's they paused, contemplating a break for some refreshment, when increased activity in the street drew their attention to the store's front glass window. At the inn opposite, the Fleece Inn, a restless team of four bay horses pranced in the morning sun. A number of passersby had quite properly stopped to admire the spirited animals.

Anne recognized the team. Despite the difference in their color in the sunlight, the horses' splendid proportions distinguished them from all others. They were unmistakably the same team she had seen in the lantern light after the dance in Hawkshead.

The carriage they pulled—large, high, and spacious—lacked decorative enamel or any distinctive crest on the door. But the coachman and grooms, though coated against the morning's chill, were handsomely outfitted in matching silver and blue livery.

Kendal endured as a major coaching stop on the route from Carlisle and points north. The town saw much traffic daily from both the movement of goods and through travelers. But even among a multitude, this splendid equipage would have drawn notice.

While Vera turned to negotiate delivery of her purchases to the Pomfrets' house, Anne remained at the window and admired the show. She expected to see the same elegantly clad lady she had glimpsed at Hawkshead. With some mixture of resentment and anxious curiosity, she wished to see the lady's face.

Instead, a familiar figure—a familiar figure with fair hair and imposing height—stepped out from under the inn's cantilevered front porch. Though he also wore a blue coat, he would never have been mistaken for one of the servants. The bustle and deference about him were for *him,* not for the carriage.

Anne watched him as though mesmerized. He looked well; he moved with vigor. He spoke to the coachman. She noticed the horses were headed south, so he had no intention of journeying back to Hawkshead, or to Wiswood, or to her. Phipps, the valet, had followed his master out of the inn. He scurried to the carriage as though the cold air out of doors might harm him, stored a small valise inside, then quickly returned to the inn. But Mr. Myles—

No, he could not be *Mister* Myles. And the lady—there was no sign of the lady. Anne wondered if she might already have boarded the coach.

"'Tis Hayden," she heard from one of the customers in the shop's doorway. "Hayden" was then murmured among the onlookers. Anne did not know the name. She knew only that it was apparently *his.*

Still she watched him. She could not help but watch him. Everyone in the shop and along the street watched him. Anne imagined that he briefly looked west, that he gave some thought to her at her home, before he at last stepped up into the coach. As it started, with a smart clatter of hooves upon the cobbles, Anne heard Vera's soft gasp behind her.

"Oh, Anne! I should have remembered! I knew I had seen him before—in London, five years ago. He was pointed out to me— at a distance, you understand—as we've just seen him. Lord Hayden! The Marquis of Hayden. Heir to the Duke of Braughton."

Anne felt the clasp of Vera's hand, but there was no warmth in it. She had never before been as grateful for the company of her friend, yet for all the comfort she felt, she might have been alone in the world—and deaf, dumb, and blind to everything but a name.

Lord Hayden. A marquis. A marquis who was destined to be

a duke. And Braughton, with those limitless properties! The incomparable wealth—

Anne turned from the window and the now empty street. Her face felt frozen as she looked at Vera. She could not seem to focus.

"Oh, Anne!" Vera repeated. "If only I had recalled! I might have spared you this."

Anne shook her head.

"It was too late." Her lips did not wish to move. "When you met him . . . it was already too late."

Chapter Ten

Braughton, the castle, commanded a gentle rise above a wide plain of fertile fields, extensive hedges, and green coppices. Centrally located in the county of Leicestershire, the castle was the seat of the Duke of Braughton, who in turn commanded not only his family but half of Leicestershire and four other counties as well. He was, in fact, widely acknowledged as one of the wealthiest men in the realm. And having diversified his holdings many years before, into much more than land, the Duke of Braughton was destined to remain so, whatever the country's current troubles.

On Hayden's arrival at the castle, which happened to be his childhood home, he was reminded that his father intended to keep the considerable Braughton fortune growing in more ways than one. His parents, it seemed, had invited two likely brides to stop over during the approach to the holidays. The two ladies— sisters—were very much alike in looks and prospective marriage portion, if not in manner. Both were Birdwistles.

Hayden's *grand-mère,* the dowager Duchess of Braughton, fumed at the presence of the young women and their parents while she herself was, as she asserted, "dying." Grand-mère accused her son the duke of cold-hearted scheming.

"He sees marriage only as the means to insure the line! He cares nothing for the heart. And you, Myles, are the same as your father!"

"Not quite, Grand-mère," he countered. "Recall that you raised Father. You must have said or done something to make him so. I was spared your iron rule."

The argument always led his *grand-mère* to shake her head in disagreement, though she would smile while doing so.

"*Non, non,* it is not so! *Lui seul le fit.* He alone did it; it is what he chose. He did not have this to follow from his parents."

"At least you admit, Grand-mère, that I have the example in mine." The point was one she could not dispute. The whole world knew that the Duke of Braughton had not married for love. Nor had His Grace, apparently, grown into it.

Hayden's *grand-mère* observed him, and as she did so, he observed her. That such a petite lady had produced such a line of tall and relatively large men always struck Hayden as incongruous. With her still richly silver head of hair, and in her elegant, beaded gown, she might have been waiting to attend a soiree, though she had kept to her own rooms for a fortnight. She had always looked quite prepared for anything. Her standards were impeccable. Despite having lived in England for more than half a century, she remained intensely French, as frequently playful as severe, and her views were still very much rooted in the last century.

Hayden had always thought her beautiful.

"You look lovely, Grand-mère."

She raised her eyebrows.

"I am suspicious, Myles, that you speak to me without sincerity. As I know, you are all too often *dégagé!*"

That she could reprove even his compliment fatigued him.

"'Twas a most genuine remark," he said, with a careless wave of his hand. "So I repeat it: You look lovely, Grand-mère."

His weary tone must have alerted her that he was in no frame of mind to be scolded. She frowned and gestured him closer to her chair by the fire. Near to, he could tell that she had not been sleeping well; there were lightly masked circles under her pale blue eyes. She looked frailer than she had even four months before.

"Why did you not stop here first on your return from Italy?" she asked. "Instead you go to see the country, to see the lakes."

"Did you miss me?"

"*Pah!* Can you not answer a question so *simple?*"

Hayden shrugged lightly. "I was not yet finished with my holiday. I wished to have a bit of sailing. And I have always enjoyed the lakes."

"Then why leave Como at all?" When he did not respond, she continued, "Perhaps you meant to flee these Birdwistles."

"Perhaps." He smiled. The manner in which his *grand-mère* pronounced *Birdwistles* amused him.

"There are too many of these girls, all with the so-silly names! Genesta, Twyla—one cannot distinguish them!"

"I would not say so. They are easy to recall. The names, that is."

His *grand-mère* prevented a smile of her own by pursing her lips.

"And now you will marry one of them, to please your father!"

"Would you not have me please him, Grand-mère?" As she looked stormy, he added, "I might hope to please myself as well. If I could only settle on one of 'em."

"Why must you marry?"

"You know why, ma'am. You yourself were obliging enough to have a son." He bowed to her. "And my mother troubled to produce two. Rather remarkable under the circumstances."

"You might leave all to David."

"Would that satisfy you, then?"

Again she looked impatient and signaled him even closer. Her assessment was difficult to bear.

"Were I to judge by your eyes, Myles, I should think you the same age as I."

"Still such a youngster?" When she gestured dismissively, he added, "The past eighteen months have been extraordinary, and extraordinarily wearin'."

"Do not give me your gammon! You have been on holiday!"

"Just so." He would not tell her of his illness. He had never told her. The news would worry her needlessly. All the same, he could not help but think of it, and of Anne Whyte, who was never far from his thoughts. Miss Whyte and her remedies, he suspected, might be most salutary for his relative.

"Are you truly unwell, Grand-mère, or do you dance too late, as you are wont to do?"

"The doctor tells me I must take care with my heart."

"Surely there is nothing new in that? We must all take care with our hearts."

Instantly her gaze was alert.

"You say this? Lord Hayden, who has not the heart?"

The charge was too much. He could bear self-denial, but not being pronounced heartless. He must at least be given credit for his few virtues.

At his offended look, she pounced, asking sharply, "What has happened?"

"Do not upset yourself, Grand-mère—"

"It upsets me to have you silent. To be kept blind! You have met a lady?"

"I have met many ladies, ma'am. Most you do not allow to be 'ladies.' "

"I interest myself only in the one who makes you look so. She is Swiss?"

"*Swiss?* Why should you think it?"

" 'Tis cold, *oui?* All those mountains! I thought such to be my punishment, a so cold and practical Swiss bride!"

Hayden shrugged, not comprehending. "I've a fondness," he drawled, "for English ladies."

"One lady."

Hayden allowed the correction with a gracious tilt of his head.

"She speaks French?" she pressed.

"She understands it. She reads Latin."

His *grand-mère's* eyebrows rose. "But she is married?"

"*Nom de nom*, Grand-mère! You think that of me?" His *grand-mère,* he noticed, looked much enlivened by this inquiry, with more color in her thin cheeks.

"I know you as I know my own heart, *mon petit.* There is some obstacle." She tapped one elegantly manicured finger against the arm of her chair. "You must paint the picture, Myles. You must describe this girl to me."

Describe Anne Whyte! He ran one hand through his hair. She had been the fresh air through the window. She had been the vista beyond. Everything about her had tantalized: her looks, her voice, her humor, the fragrance of her skin and clothes—all of her ubiquitous herbs . . .

He felt his waistcoat pocket, where he had tucked one of the last horehound drops. He hoarded it, like a talisman, to keep him safe and sane. Parting from her had made clear how poorly he bore it.

The dowager Duchess of Braughton looked expectant.

"She is very bright," he said at last.

"Bright? *Comment? Intelligente?*"

"*Oui, mais aussi . . . Elle est—illuminante.*"

"*Un diamant?*"

"*De première eau.*" He sighed, then paced. "She is not of town, Grand-mère, but if she were—there is no question . . . She holds every gaze. I tell you, 'twas something to see their faces! The vicar told me she is 'adored,' and the reason for it . . . But she would be adored anywhere, and perhaps even without reason—" At his *grand-mère*'s amused expression, he recollected himself. "Her eyes are gray. Not always the same shade of gray. They . . . shine," he said with an effort. "Her complexion is fair and healthy and—*bright*." He passed a hand over his eyes; the memory hurt him. "She is day to my night. And as unreachable."

"*Porquoi?* Why—why should this be? What makes you turn from her, and consider the Birdwistle? Your so luminous girl, she is not a gentlewoman?"

"She is. She is. None more so." He looked away and out the window, to the formal gardens on the south side of the castle. He had sent a letter to Everett Whyte from Penrith, complimenting the first-volume history and assuring him that the second volume would shortly claim his attention. Hayden had thanked Whyte for his hospitality, but he had declined to include a payment, judging that such remuneration would be deemed an insult.

Both the Whytes were very proud. Despite his commendation, and his thanks, and his frankness—late as it came—he considered it likely that neither father nor daughter would ever forgive him for his deception.

His *grand-mère* had quietly observed him.

"Myles, *mon cher*," she said. "You know that you have a heritage in France, a long and rich heritage."

"It faltered, dear lady, when you abandoned it."

She brushed the compliment aside.

"That heritage—it is now gone. After so much of the change—*la Révolution, l'empereur!* But listen—this legacy, it was not lost to you—or to others—because a marquis married below his rank. *Tout le contraire.*"

"You speak of grave matters indeed," he said, conscious of echoing Anne Whyte. "And you argue well, Grand-mère. But this is Braughton in the balance. I shouldn't wish to exaggerate, but I cannot claim to be just *any* marquis."

She offered him a frail hand, which he took and gently saluted.

"*Mon pauvre petit,*" she murmured. "You must still be permitted to choose."

"Do not pity me, Grand-mère. The constraints are largely of my making. And I have not treated her well."

"If she loves, she will forgive. You must make her love you."

Hayden smiled. "She is as stubborn as you are, Grand-mère."

"So?" she asked imperiously, "Even *I* love. It is not to be thought, that this girl should not want *mon petit-fils!*"

Myles left her then, because she had said what she wanted to say, and because she tired. But speaking of Anne Whyte had, most unexpectedly, lightened his heart. His next interview, with his father, loomed as less of a trial. There was no question, however, that the Duke of Braughton could seem most imposing, even to his exceptionally confident son.

"I understand," his father said, showing him into his office, a room on the north side of the castle, and thus inevitably dark and chilly, "that you resolved the problems in Cumberland to everyone's satisfaction?"

"You had the note from Munroe, then? I thought he would prefer to write it. He was concerned that you might find his own role less than exemplary."

"In all honesty, Hayden, he should have had instinct enough to suspect something was wrong at Hollen. You think I should keep him on?"

Hayden had expected the question. The duke demanded much from those representing him.

"I do think you should keep Munroe, sir," he said. "Wenfield's would have been a difficult scheme for anyone to uncover. There was nothing on paper, nothing in the books, only the word of the tenants. And that letter—"

"I have never liked Wenfield."

"No, Father. I know you have not. Yet he has some qualities even you would admire."

The Duke of Braughton looked skeptical.

"Pray tell me again, why do we not prosecute? I do not question your choice, of course. But even Munroe argued for more of a penalty. And the steward, Greeley, must be held to account."

"I had a personal interest, Father."

"In Wenfield? I am astonished."

"Not in Wenfield. You recall that suggestions in one letter originally led to your concern? You mentioned it this past summer, without a great deal of urgency. But 'twas one of the reasons I traveled north to survey matters. As it happened, I did not wish the author of that letter—Mr. Whyte—or his family to suffer for it." Hayden pulled Whyte's missive from his coat and handed it to his father. Braughton took it over to the lamp on his desk to read.

"'Tis both rational and eloquent," he said. "This E. Whyte has decided rhetorical skills."

"Yes, I think so."

"Will *he* be satisfied with this outcome, d'you think?"

"He should be. Though I suspect it is not in the man's nature to rest on his laurels."

"You know him?"

"I do, sir. This is not the only letter he has penned."

His father's gaze narrowed at the admission. "'Tis amazing," he said, "that a mere mister might cause so much fuss."

"If not *cause*"—Hayden smiled—"he certainly *forwards* it. He is an Englishman, Father. And quite determined to challenge for 'justice.' A reformer. A judicious gentleman as well, apparently, for he not only pens the complaints but writes separately, offering to mediate! His dissenting opinions, however, do not appear to extend to the church."

"He must take care not to go too far. I suspect he's the one who has Ambrose erupting about 'threats.' If you know the man, you might put a word in his ear."

Ambrose as well! Hayden grimaced. And here he had believed himself comprehensive in sending half a dozen notes from Penrith, including one to his friend Leigh-Maitland, now Lord Tinsdale.

"I asked you to address this matter, Hayden," his father said. "And you must continue to do as you judge best. But I recommend you arrange some post for him."

"For Mr. Whyte?"

Braughton nodded. "Make him a magistrate. There is always an opening, given the usual attrition and the need to replace those who prove less than capable. Let us see how Mr. Whyte's sense of justice preserves order. Let him be a free thinker with a different brief. Within a year, we might recommend that he be knighted. I shall alert Trevelyan." He leaned to scribble a note for his secretary. "Service to the nation, et cetera. Ironically, 'tis what *Wenfield* most wanted. 'Twas writ large on that scoundrel. And now Whyte, who does not seek it, shall have it."

"Mr. Whyte might not accept the offer of a position. He may object to the required oaths or to being identified too closely with authority."

"Then he would be so entirely unlike other gentlemen that I do not understand him." His Grace flashed a rare smile.

Hayden smiled in turn. "I believe you would admire Everett Whyte, sir."

"I imagine that I might. He is what we would all be were we not burdened by obligations. There is certainly something renewing in it. The man has a youngster's heart. But there is also a threshold for everyone. He must think of his situation and his family."

The comment reminded Hayden uncomfortably of their houseguests and of a topic on which he had never had easy discourse with his parent.

"About the Birdwistles," he began.

"Shall one of them suit you, then?" His father's expression

lightened. "I understand the eldest has had an interest in you for some time."

"I honor her persistence, sir." Every season for a decade, Avis Birdwistle had signaled her preference, forever gazing at him much too significantly. "But I've no wish to succumb to it."

"Well, then—the younger girl is prettier."

"There is nothing behind Miss Oribelle's eyes, Father. I fear I cannot wed a simpleton."

His father sighed. "Your birthday is this month, Myles. Surely after thirty-two years on this earth, you know what suits you?"

"I understand what is owed the family, sir. Though David is already married. And likely to present you with a grandchild in the near term."

"Barring a misfortune—and heaven forbid that anything should happen to you, Myles—David should not have to interrupt his life to live yours. He has given enough."

Hayden agreed. He had always accepted his role. Whether it qualified as a "life" was another matter.

"I know my duty, sir."

"And you have done well. I am conscious of it."

"Thank you, Father."

"So this one small item should not prove too arduous. The Birdwistles are of an old, illustrious line. Any one of the ladies brings connection and fortune."

"Surely we do not need either?"

"Need? Certainly not, but 'tis expected. Why should you not welcome both? Miss Birdwistle and her sister are good-tempered and not ill favored. The family is prolific."

"For females, Father." Both of them smiled fleetingly. Myles had viewed marriage as onerous, to be sure, but a duty like any other. Now, knowing he desired better made the prospect a punishment.

The duke's gaze became most penetrating.

"What troubles you, Myles?"

"If I were to marry Avis Birdwistle"—even proposing as much made him swallow—"I would never love her."

His father looked down. His features still held the ghost of their shared smile, but now the smile appeared stiff. He took a moment before speaking.

"Then, do not," he said at last.

Hayden hesitated. "Do not love her?"

His father's gaze again met his. He shook his head. "I should have thought my meaning clear. Do not marry her."

"But I thought—"

"You thought me such an ogre? Myles, if you know *that*—and you know it *now*—you would be surrendering too much. And you would only recognize the impossibility if you have chosen another." When Hayden remained silent, he asked, "Tell me, does Mr. Wenfield have a daughter?"

"No. Wenfield has a son. Mr. Whyte has a daughter."

The Duke of Braughton's eyebrows rose. "I suggest you move quickly, then. The Marquis of Hayden might marry where he will, but choosing the daughter of a man who courts being transported is not good sense. Had you been less lovestruck, you would have been thinking more clearly."

"Miss Whyte still may not have me."

His father looked incredulous. "Then *she* would be so entirely unlike other ladies . . ."

Hayden smiled. "I will act promptly, Father. But first, it seems the Birdwistles must hear *two* items of unwelcome news. For they have just lost a daughter to an elopement, and I suspect they cannot know it."

"I happily leave our houseguests to you, Hayden. Mr. Birdwistle overwhelms me."

Hayden was still smiling as he returned to the main rooms. Marriage, which had threatened for too long, now promised only pleasure. That his father should have yielded astonished him, as it would no doubt please Grand-mère. With Braughton's permission, Hayden now felt only an impatience to act, to be getting on. But first, there were the Birdwistles.

As he entered the morning salon, he thought the family must just have heard his step. The four Birdwistles stood uncharacteristically silent by the door to the terrace, though he had heard their conversation as he approached.

He had not seen them on his arrival the previous night; he

had been very late and had rushed upstairs to check on his ailing *grand-mère* before she retired. So the Birdwistles, who had
most pointedly stopped to see *him,* in hopes that they would all
shortly mean much more to one another, were very eager to
entertain him.

Hayden knew they would not be as eager to hear his report.

"How was your visit on the Continent, Lord Hayden?"
Mr. Birdwistle asked affably. "We occasionally read news of
you."

"Did you, sir? That is a surprise, as I do not recall doin' anything worthy of note."

"Oh, the *smallest* items reach the papers," Miss Oribelle assured him, no doubt intending to compliment him. Hayden had
judged her to be about nineteen. Her sister Avis, the eldest, he
knew to be in her late twenties. Though they looked like all the
Birdwistles, a deal of difference lay in their comportment; Miss
Birdwistle's demeanor was as matronly as her mother's, while
Miss Oribelle enthused like a child.

"I have not been in Europe these past two or three weeks,
Miss Oribelle, but up in the north, tending to some estate matters."

"How thrilling!"

Mrs. Birdwistle quickly asked about his *grand-mère*'s health.
He told them that Grand-mère was on the mend, though he silently allowed that his elderly relative might only have looked
considerably better after hearing of Anne Whyte.

Which thought reminded him of his purpose.

"I did not have opportunity to tell you last night, as I was so
late gettin' in, but your daughter, Miss Elissa, is most certainly
wed by now."

They looked shocked. Hayden knew instantly that the Birdwistles had not even supposed that Elissa's sentiments were so
violent. They were, as Hayden had told Henry Purvis, a most
respectable family. Given their reaction, he now doubted they
would have stopped at Braughton even a second had they known.

Miss Birdwistle quickly settled her stricken mother upon a
close, supportive sofa. Mr. Birdwistle turned an interesting
shade, one that Hayden would have likened to fuchsia. As

complicated as his own future appeared, Hayden could not envy Henry Purvis.

"Who is the—the—" Birdwistle struggled to say *gentleman.*

"Mr. Henry Purvis. I saw them just shy of Gretna, sir. They were both in good spirits. They intended to return to you immediately. In fact, they might be at your doorstep by now. Berkshire, isn't it?"

"Return to us!" Birdwistle spluttered. "They certainly shall not!"

Hayden signaled a footman to hurry some refreshments.

"We had just recently left my sister to stay with friends in Yorkshire, Lord Hayden," Avis Birdwistle said. "This is a very great surprise."

"And why 'Lissa should be the first to wed!" Miss Oribelle wailed. "It is not fair!"

"Hush, child, hush," Mrs. Birdwistle managed. With a trembling hand, she accepted a glass of lemonade.

"You do not know Mr. Purvis?" Hayden asked. "His father is Earl of—"

"His father might be king of all the world!" Birdwistle fumed. "But *he* is a knave, a scamp, a penniless, thankless ne'er-do-well! I refused him her hand, and *this* is what he does! I shall never speak to them again!"

"Papa," Miss Birdwistle said. Hayden had to admire her calm—or possibly she remained unmoved. "Elissa was much taken with Mr. Purvis—"

"And now she is taken *by* him! So be it. She is no daughter of mine!"

For no reason apparent to Hayden, Miss Oribelle chose to cry. He found the girl a seat but approached Mrs. Birdwistle rather than tend the youngster.

"I wish you would not look upon this so unfavorably, ma'am," he said. "The manner of their marriage leaves something to be desired, 'tis true. But the Purvis family is almost as illustrious as your own. Though he does not inherit, Mr. Purvis is not without friends. He will have prospects"—Hayden knew he himself was bound to supply them—"and he and Miss Elissa are a most devoted couple."

Mrs. Birdwistle appeared to be recovering. Perhaps she realized that having one of her many daughters wed, and to an "honorable," was much to be preferred.

Miss Avis Birdwistle's gaze settled disturbingly on Hayden. "I did not know you were romantic, my lord," she said, with such an openly suggestive look that he was taken aback. Miss Birdwistle had, heretofore, always proved powerfully composed.

"Perhaps because I am not," he told her firmly. Her expression instantly crumpled, into one so pinched and despairing that he felt some remorse. He had given her no cause for disappointment. But he silently allowed that had he not fallen ill, had he not journeyed to the Lakes, had he never met Anne Whyte, he would have resigned himself to offering for Miss Birdwistle. He satisfied his conscience, however, by affirming that the very attributes that had made her so perennially eligible for *him* would soon see her wed to another.

He did wonder whether he could truthfully deny being *romantic,* when he knew himself to be as lovestruck as his father had charged. But he considered his rebuttal a reasonably gentle means of dousing Miss Birdwistle's expectations.

"We must—" Her mother rallied, with a beseeching look at her glowering husband. "Mr. Birdwistle, we truly must return home at once."

"You needn't do so on our account, ma'am, I am sure," Hayden offered. "Although I myself leave for the north tomorrow morning."

"But you have just returned!" Miss Oribelle protested.

"So I have, Miss Oribelle. But I left one important item unaddressed. I assure you, the matter is pressing." He turned to Birdwistle. "Might I say, sir, that Mr. and Mrs. Purvis will always be welcome here at Braughton, and at the house in town? I think you will find they make a most agreeable pair."

Birdwistle's frown eased, though it did not disappear. "I thank you, my lord," he said heavily. "Godspeed."

And with hopes that would indeed be the case, and after taking leave of the ladies, Hayden hurried upstairs to alert Grandmère to his plans.

Chapter Eleven

Anne, who was determined never to forgive Lord Hayden, nevertheless decided to keep his iniquity a secret from her father. She nursed her outrage privately for less than a day, however, for on her return home from Kendal, her father summoned her to his study, where he sat waving a letter above his desk.

"He is a marquis, Anne. Our Mr. Myles is Lord Hayden, Marquis of Hayden, son of the Duke of Braughton." His expression conveyed little to Anne—not anger or surprise, or even excitement.

"Yes, I—I knew."

"Did you? He told you and swore you to secrecy?"

Anne shook her head. "Vera and I just recently observed him by chance in Kendal. The crowd there knew his name."

Her father eyed her closely.

"He makes you unhappy."

"He lied to us. I make *myself* unhappy thinking of him at all."

"Perhaps there was some misunderstanding, as he was ill."

"No, Father. He deliberately withheld his identity from us."

"He might have had a reason."

"What would that be?"

"I cannot imagine. But he did strike me as a most eminently rational man. Would you have withheld treatment for the fellow"—he smiled—"knowing he was a peer?"

"Certainly not! But I should have been more discreet."

"You are always discreet, my dear. I am convinced you must have nothing to regret. Unlike your father, who recalls holding

150

forth in his usual expansive manner." He smiled. "As it is, no lasting damage has been done. The tone of this missive is distinctly friendly. I do not believe he shall have the constables after me."

Anne frowned. Where before she would have known he was joking, she now wondered whether his activities did indeed skirt the edge of legality. That he should mention constables alarmed her.

As much as she now disdained Lord Hayden, she granted that at least he had not continued his ruse. He had sent his apology from Penrith, before departing for Kendal and his home in Leicestershire. But he had also, too clearly in her view, had no intention of returning to Wiswood.

She stood very straight and focused on her father.

"When you mention constables, Father, I wish I might believe you are teasing. You tell me not to worry about these letters of yours. But you must see that it concerns me greatly. I shouldn't like to have my father heading for prison—or worse." She had not meant to sound such a scold, but some combination of exhaustion and disappointment made her shrewish.

"Why, Anne! This is not like you. Did our mysterious marquis make promises to you, that you should snap so?"

"Might we keep to the problem of constables, Father? I find I can only deal with one gentleman at a time."

Her father looked his surprise.

"I do humbly beg your pardon, Anne. You have expressed concern before about the letters—perhaps rightly, though I believe they have always been respectful in tone. You must read them if you wish; they are none of them long." He unlocked one drawer of his desk. Pulling out a tied, flat box of correspondence, he placed it before her.

"Father, I don't—I truly do not wish to read them."

"I assure you, you shall not be judged a conspirator."

She blushed. "That never occurred to me! Only—do tell me—did you write to the Duke of Braughton?"

He nodded. "And to Tinsdale, Ambrose, Lyndon, the Earl of Grantham, Blenhallow, Colworth, Humphrey-Brown, Barrett,

Skevers—all of them. Some attempt changes, Anne. Whether this correspondence played some small part, spurring them to closer and more responsible attention, I do not know."

"And how long have you been sending these letters, sir?"

"Just since this past summer, when difficulties seemed to strike the hardest. There would have been little need before."

"I do not ask you to stop writing, Father, only to have a care. Were one of these powerful landowners to summon you, to charge you, and have you imprisoned, I should not know how to get on."

"I would dispute that most vigorously, my dear, as I have every faith that you might manage superbly without your Papa. Indeed, perhaps too well for my taste! But as it happens, my letter-writing days may have come to a close."

"Why, Father?"

"Because of one I have received." Again he waved Lord Hayden's missive. "I believe his lordship wishes to be forgiven, daughter. And he would not care, if he did not *care*—if you understand me." As she blushed, he asked gently, "Do you care, Anne?"

"I may have thought I did, sir, before all of his . . . before his misleading conduct."

"His misleading conduct was ongoing, yet you apparently did consider him before his real name was revealed to you. Would you have encouraged him, had he remained *Mr. Myles?*"

"That is such a supposition." She drew breath. "Sometimes we imagine things that are not so, and create a fancy. Mr. Myles—Lord Hayden—was only ever proper—" But even as she said it, Anne recalled his last kiss upon her hand. With the memory, her fingers clenched protectively.

"Then I am disappointed in him."

"Father! You cannot mean you would have had me *dangling* after Lord Hayden?"

He smiled. "No. I should have had him dangling after *you*. Most every other gentleman of our acquaintance has. His lordship cannot be exempt. Why should my splendid Anne not be a marchioness? And she would make an incomparable duchess. That is one way to reform the lot, certainly!" He chuckled at the thought. "Had our patient simply overstepped, I would be writing a different type of letter."

"I shall not . . . I shall not stay to listen to this, Papa! That you would *prefer* to have had me *compromised!* 'Twill not be the constables who come for you, but the porters from Bedlam."

With a great deal of pride and a very warm face, she turned to leave him, only to hear him say,

"He promises to return, Anne." As she looked back, her father again waved the letter. "He promises to return. And then what shall you say to him?"

"I shall tell him that *you* might forgive him, but that I never shall."

She sought refuge in her workroom. She had intended to fashion congratulatory gifts for Vera, but instead chose to pummel dried gentian root to powder for bitters, a task that more directly suited her state of mind.

At least she now understood his allusion to the need to "make amends." How cryptic he had been! Obviously much indulged, he was also, contrarily, a most disciplined gentleman. She wondered if he had always expected to explain himself. And though he had played a matchlessly cool game, she still felt a fool.

Her memory, unbidden, replayed those instances in which he had appeared too comfortable, even bored, with town ways. To someone less naive than Anne Whyte, such easy references would have indicated his familiarity with the first circles of society. On the trip back from Kendal, and now in the privacy of her home, she had had time to catalog those moments in which he might have revealed himself, but had chosen not to. Soon after his arrival, he had asked to be called merely "Myles," a request even more forward than she had imagined at the time. And when he had taken his leave in Hawkshead last Saturday night, he had quite deliberately called her "Anne."

She had been touched by the informality, but now found it impudent. He had not behaved as properly as he ought, because he had clearly been privileged to behave only as he *chose.*

If he returned—and she fought any expectation at the thought— she would make her displeasure quite clear to him.

Anne supposed she should tell Vera of Lord Hayden's

letter—that he had troubled to reveal his stratagem—but she was strangely reluctant to interrupt her aggrieved solitude. She hoped her father would say nothing of their former guest's identity, but she knew that he, like Vera, would see no reason to keep mum. Their little world here in the vale of Esthwaite was bound to resonate with the news for months.

At dinner, she and her father maintained polite conversation on every topic but one. That her parent appeared to be in particularly contented spirits, Anne attributed to his satisfaction with the progress he made on his history, not to any amusement at her own carefully controlled manner. Her father, she thought, might imagine what he would of Lord Hayden's interests. Anne could only recall the unknown lady at the inn, and imagine something completely different.

She found confirmation of this view the following week, when Perry Wenfield again came to call.

"He is Lord Hayden, Anne! Myles Trent, Marquis of Hayden. I'd heard of him in town, of course, but never met him. Some call him 'His Resplendence,' though I cannot see that there is anything so splendid about him, except his capacity to lie!" As Perry sneered, his face flushed. "He's played havoc with Father, who must now leave Hollen Hall, all because of some misunderstanding over the rents! Father says he has no doubt 'tis personal reprisal of some sort; he's always felt the duke—of Braughton, that is, Hayden's father—never liked him, and now just simply wants him gone. Father won't tell me any more about the matter. He has his pride, doesn't he? But I suspect Braughton, and Hayden too, have concocted some story to suit themselves. My parents leave for Barbados, sailing from Liverpool, in days. Mother wants the sun, you see."

He paused only for a deep breath, then plunged on.

"Oh, I shan't be out more than a month's income, as I've my own money from my aunt and shall have Mama's portion. Father says there may not be anything else to inherit. But what do I need with that? I've offered to make some of my own over to Father, but he won't have it. This Hayden is a blackguard for bringing him down like this, I can tell you."

"But Mr. Wenfield," Anne interrupted, having listened to him with much incomprehension. "I do not understand you. Did Mr. Myles—did Lord Hayden have no reason, other than some petty animosity, for asking your parents to leave Hollen?"

"No reason at all, I tell you! Father says the agent, Munroe, got things wrong, that monies rightly due from the tenants are being held against Father! These puffed-up peers might do as they like, Anne. Father was that close"—Perry held two fingers up a half inch apart—"to being knighted. And now he's banished to Barbados."

Anne still doubted that she understood.

"Surely, given such an injustice, your father must go to the courts?"

Perry Wenfield shook his artfully tousled head and started to pace.

"Father will not have Mother bear it. D'you know Mama has said scarcely a word these past ten days? She had come to think of Hollen as home. After so much time, even moving to an estate of their own would have been trying enough. But Barbados! Of course Father is concerned that he might appear to have been let to bail, as though *he* has done something wrong, when there's not one bit of proof against him. Mind you, that's why Hayden came calling, full of bluster and threat! Because he knew they would never prove anything at court."

"I am . . . I am amazed, Mr. Wenfield," Anne managed. She was thinking that her father's letters of complaint were, perhaps, very necessary indeed, if this were the manner in which tenants were treated by the higher ranks. "How do they hope to attract a new tenant to Hollen after this?"

"I haven't a clue. And let me tell you, I haven't a care, either! If *this* is the way they tend their properties," he said contemptuously, "we are better out of it."

"Mr. Wenfield, I am so sorry."

He now flung his hat, which he had been waving about since his arrival, onto a chair.

"Never mind that now. You needn't be sorry for *me,* I assure you. I still have means, and I choose *you,* Anne."

His persistence appalled her, particularly under the circumstances.

"You honor me, Mr. Wenfield. But it makes no difference."

"Do you say so, sweet?" He grinned broadly. "I knew you would be constant!"

"You do not let me finish, Mr. Wenfield! I would not marry you before, and I will not now. I fear you are greatly agitated by these events, with the Hall and your parents and Mr. . . . Lord Hayden. I fear you cannot know your own mind. But I certainly know mine."

Perry pouted, then began to pace.

"I have been most clear in *my* mind, Anne, for some time. And you must know that before *he* came, you were wont to give me every indication of interest!"

"I must dispute that, Mr. Wenfield. I gave you no more 'indication of interest' than I give daily, in friendship, to any one of my neighbors."

"You danced with me twice at Peabody's ball!"

"I danced twice with several other gentlemen. I am not planning to wed any of them."

For a moment he looked confused; then he scowled.

"Perhaps you consider attaching one with whom you danced only *once?*"

"I believe I have told you before, Mr. Wenfield. I do not have any thought of marriage!"

"Which is probably a good thing," he countered angrily, "since *he* will certainly never think of it! He would scoff at such a hope as disgustingly forward." His glance slid significantly, and most hurtfully, to her lamed side.

"I cannot think whom you mean."

"Hayden! Blast him! Your patient. The posing peer!"

"Since I have no thought to attach Lord Hayden, he cannot believe me forward."

"Oh, you do sound so *reasonable,* Anne Whyte! But I see it in your eyes. You've not been the same since he came. I've wondered what it was. You haven't a clue, have you, about the speculation. All the talk! That he's made, and won, extravagant wagers; that he's been *dueling!* He was even engaged, Anne—to his brother's wife! And now there's talk he has a years-long understanding with some high-and-mighty heiress. He's no paragon. I have just as much right to you as he—more so! And he shan't have you!"

He lunged for her in such a startling, unprecedented manner that Anne, still stung by the references to Hayden's doings, was caught up in his clasp in a second and hardly aware of how she had come to be there. She stared at his chin, then into his eyes, then pushed hard against his chest.

"Do stop this, Mr. Wenfield," she said, furious at her inability to dissuade the man. "My father will hear of your behavior!"

"Yes, he shall—when I ask for your hand! You should have permitted me to do so before, Anne. We've wasted too much time." As he moved to kiss her, Anne thrust very hard with two fists against his chest. She prevented his kiss but could not entirely evade his arms, which still caught her around the waist.

"Oh dear." A familiar drawl, a painfully familiar drawl, had them turning together toward the door. "We intrude. Am I to congratulate you, Wenville?"

Lord Hayden stood in the entry hall, accompanied by another fashionably dressed gentleman, a stranger. A gaping Molly hovered behind them.

Flushed from her efforts to escape, Anne could only stare at Hayden. She had not heard a carriage; she had heard no knock or conversation; she had been intent on parrying Mr. Wenfield. That superior drawl had just asked her something—*congratulations?*

"No." "Yes." She and Perry spoke at once. Lord Hayden's answering smile was humorless. He swung his greatcoat off in one smooth movement and passed it behind him to Molly.

"We must leave you to sort yourselves out." His gaze settled on Perry Wenfield's lingering embrace, just as Perry's arms dropped abruptly from her waist. "But before doin' so, might I present Lord Tinsdale to you, Miss Whyte?"

Anne stumbled into some semblance of a curtsy. This stranger, the new Lord Tinsdale, was the landowner with the largest holdings in the area. Anne felt her face flame. Hayden had pointedly presented Lord Tinsdale to *her*—a very great elevation for any country miss and a distinction that she did not deserve.

"Lord Tinsdale," she said. "You are welcome."

The earl bowed neatly and looked to Wenfield, but Hayden made no move to introduce Perry to Tinsdale, a snub that Perry clearly understood. He glared at Hayden and, without taking his leave of Anne, strode past them and on out the door.

"Miss Whyte, we are here to see your father," Hayden said.

Anne could not quite bring her gaze to his.

"Yes, of course." She led the way to her father's library, tapped on the open door, and after announcing the visitors hastened to remove herself. As Lord Hayden brushed past her into the library, Anne was too aware of him—of his size, of his scent—and too aware of her own absurd discomposure. She made a point of smiling brightly at Lord Tinsdale.

She asked Simmons to attend the gentlemen with some refreshments and, after dismissing goggling Molly, returned alone to the drawing room. Perry had left his hat. She could not abide even that reminder of the recent spectacle, so she picked it up and crumpled it carelessly into a bureau drawer.

She wanted only to hide upstairs. But if her father could entertain these two noblemen, who had every reason to believe themselves injured by his letters, Anne felt she could face one who had so unfeelingly injured *her*.

Out the window facing the road, she could now see the horses the gentlemen had ridden, the animals being walked by the two grooms who had charge of them. Young Tim skipped along beside them, talking animatedly to the grooms, no doubt quizzing these august personages about their duties. The little hamlet of Wiswood rarely saw so much excitement. Anne knew she must deal in future with the repercussions of *this* visit as well as the last.

For a moment, she wished life might return to its simpler predictabilities of just a few weeks ago, before Lord Hayden had been brought to her home. But even as she wished it, footsteps at the entrance to the drawing room intruded on her reverie. As she looked to the doorway, Anne decided that Lord Hayden's smile did not reach his eyes.

"You are alone?" he asked.

"As you see, *my lord*." His eyebrows rose. He would have to have been deaf not to catch her emphasis. "You are also alone?"

"Tinsdale and your father had a few specifics to work through, a discussion to which I would have contributed little." He paused, and looked so set and grim that Anne instantly feared for her father.

When Hayden stepped farther into the room, she said quickly, in a flooding failure of pride, "Lord Hayden, my lord. For my father, I must ask of your station, of your influence, of your understanding . . ." She broke off. A few days before, she would have felt entirely comfortable in asking much of him—indeed, she *had* asked much of him—but no longer.

"Miss Whyte, you needn't ask. You need never have asked. Your father was so generous to me, that I can be no less to him."

"But the letters—"

"Were perhaps ill-advised. But they are not threatening, nor truly actionable. There is nothing to prevent him from accepting our offer. And he has, apparently, accepted it."

"Your offer?"

"Mr. Whyte has agreed to accept a position as a magistrate, to take Sir Ogden Berry's post. Sir Ogden, as I hear it, has not been up to the task."

"But Father is not a lawyer—"

"Many are not. One cannot dispute that your father knows the law as well as any, though he is unlikely to be constrained by it."

She thought his small smile disturbingly intimate. "And you say he has agreed?"

"Yes. He chooses to exert his considerable energy in this new endeavor. He proposes to rein in some of his principles, for your sake, Miss Whyte."

"For my sake!" Anne eyed him. He looked magnificent, in some handsome combination of blue and gray: coat, waistcoat, breeches, boots . . . She could not seem to focus on any one article. She wondered how she could ever have mistaken him for anything but what he was.

She raised her chin. "My father does not know what you've done to the Wenfields!"

"I have done nothing to Mr. Wenfield, when, as it happens, he deserved much. That is the problem."

Anne could not interpret his intent look.

"His son, Mr. Perry Wenfield, has just been telling me of your injustice—of your false charges, of your groundless and heartless *eviction* of his parents!"

"He said all that? And here I thought him more agreeably occupied."

She gestured dismissively, though the comment brought the blood to her cheeks.

"I have been hearing much of you, Lord Hayden."

"I venture to say that you *knew* much more of me, Miss Whyte, than anything you have heard since. I am the same."

"Are you? Oh, I knew you were a gambler, though not to such extremes. But did I know you had dueled?"

"I have not dueled."

"Did I know you were engaged—to your *brother's wife?*"

"She was not then his wife. And I had no intention of marryin' her."

"And *that* must absolve you? I suppose one might cast facts as one wishes. It is all in the perception!"

"I should not have thought you more cynical than I, Miss Whyte." He looked more forbearing than angry. "These matters are easily explained."

"And your *masquerade* in this house. What was that about then, *Mister Myles?*"

"I was not myself."

"Do you mean to jest?"

Something implacably cool settled about his expression.

"I must rely on your honesty, Miss Whyte. I believe I was feverish. Certainly you insisted on telling me so, as an excuse to force endless grassy swill down my throat."

"*Swill?*" Her lips firmed. "I am sorry I wasted it on you. I believe I preferred you ill!"

"You might satisfy yourself, then, that I am unlikely to recover from my present affliction." At her puzzled frown, he shrugged. "I never intended to sport with you. I was on the point of telling you my full name when Mr. Perry Wenfield came to call."

"And why should Mr. Wenfield's visit have changed anything?"

"Indeed." His examination of her face unnerved her. "Why should it? I must ask you, Miss Whyte—am I to wish you happy?"

Happy? How could he think it a possibility?

"That is . . . that is none of your concern."

"I think you will find that I have made it my concern." He had not looked away from her. "Shall you wed him?"

"He has offered. I have not decided . . . upon my response."

He sighed. "If I advise you that you might do better, you shall elope with him this instant. Yes, I know this of your temper, ma'am." He held her angry gaze. "As his offer stands, and as I interrupted, I shan't press. But Miss Whyte"—he tendered the thin packet of documents he had been holding—"you must have these. You used to trust me once. I do hope you will trust me again." Her gaze fell from his. She scarcely noticed the letters he handed to her. "We have told your father that his message was received. I've requested more—from Lyndon, Grantham, others. You needn't worry."

"Favors . . . ," she said, with a catch in her throat.

"If you like." Again he shrugged. "'Tis connection. 'Tis politics." His easy confidence seemed to heighten the absence of her own.

Her father and Lord Tinsdale had crossed the front hall. Anne swiftly hid the letters against the folds of her skirt.

"My dear," her father said, stepping toward her with the broadest of smiles, "you will scarcely credit this—"

But he had no chance to test her. She muttered an inarticulate excuse and, hurrying past their guests, fled the room.

Chapter Twelve

I shan't require your bays from you, after all, Hayden. 'Tis compensation enough to see you so disordered! I shall dine well on this tale for months. What a pity Knowles ain't around to embellish it." Tony Leigh-Maitland, Lord Tinsdale, grinned so expansively that Hayden was tempted to deprive him of teeth.

"Before you grow too pleased with yourself, Tinsdale, best be certain you can afford to spurn the cattle. Given the arrangements to satisfy Whyte and his constituents, you will not be as plump in the pockets as you were yesterday."

"You did argue this outlay as a matter of insurance, my friend. Or was it more truly the blackmail I suspected?" Again Tinsdale grinned. "I believe you said concessions now would be for the good of the realm, and spare me the horror of having enraged workmen trash the family pile. Was that not the case?"

"I'll not repeat myself."

"No, you rarely do." Tinsdale laughed. "I should dearly like to know what you intend to reap from this, though. I understand why you should be in such a dark mood. The lovely Miss Whyte appears to have bestowed her affections elsewhere."

"That is enough." Hayden's lips set grimly. "And if you broadcast one word regarding Miss Whyte, I shall call you out."

Tinsdale merely smiled and settled silently and comfortably in his saddle.

They said not one word more until they reached Hawkshead, where Hayden and his party had put up at the inn. The bay horses, which Hayden had traded to Tinsdale for his prompt compliance, were safely stabled after a fleet and furious journey north.

The rush had been foolhardy, Hayden thought now, and only to find disappointment.

The scene in the Whytes' drawing room had unmanned him.

Tinsdale claimed to need a rest and a wash and a chance to warm himself by the inn's fire after a chilly day's travel. Hayden, too, found the prospect welcome. He would think more clearly once Phipps arranged for a bath, once he had changed these worn clothes, once he was more properly himself.

Again he fingered the herb lozenge in his waistcoat pocket. He had not yet done with Perry Wenfield. Indeed, Hayden thought there was much left unfinished. But perhaps he was the only one to think so.

It had snowed lightly the night before; the heights around the valley were capped in white. Shaded corners in the village still held remnants of icy frosting. Hayden looked out pensively from his window at the inn. He was unlikely to visit the area again for a very long while—if the next day did not bring a change. Everett Whyte had invited them to supper the following evening, Sunday, and Hayden still intended to go—to see Anne Whyte one last time, if for no other reason.

For a moment, he wished he might have someone to consult. Tinsdale, though a good sort and a reliable friend, was too pleased with the situation by half; he could not provide worthy counsel. Hayden suspected, rather dourly, that this hand would have to be played out in a solitary fashion, as his own instincts, and Anne Whyte's preferences, dictated.

Disheartened, he set about his bath.

When he and Tinsdale entered the Blue Duck's spacious taproom later that afternoon, the pub was already filling with patrons, though an hour or more of workable light remained. At one of the tables, Perry Wenfield sat with a tankard. Failing to spot him, even in such a large and busy room, would have been impossible.

"Lord Tinsdale!" Mrs. Midgeley, the proprietor, greeted Tinsdale with a smile and a quick bob. "And Mr. Myles! I'd not expected you back!" She frowned. "I've let that room out . . ."

"Do not trouble yourself, good lady," Hayden said. "I am stopping at the inn with a larger party, and just for the night."

"Mrs. Midgeley, your 'Mr. Myles' here is Lord Hayden," Tinsdale relayed to her, with a wink at Hayden.

"Is he? M'lord," she corrected, bobbing again before gesturing them toward a table some twenty feet across from Wenfield. "Lost a relation, then, like Lord Tinsdale here, I take it?" She did not require an answer. "I'm right sorry that t'other must have died, and only this past week, too! Will you—"

"Is this Mr. Wenfield, Mrs. Midgeley?" Tinsdale asked as they passed Perry's table, thus eliciting the introduction Hayden had denied him just two hours before. Hayden knew Tinsdale was more likely to desire entertainment than to wish to make amends for the earlier slight.

Perry Wenfield's sulky expression did not alter, even as Mrs. Midgeley warmly presented him. He shot Hayden an angry look and mumbled only the merest courtesies to Tinsdale. Hayden wondered why the youngster should be drowning his sorrows, a state which should more rightly belong to *him*.

As they crossed to their table and took their seats, Hayden recognized a few other faces, men whom he had last seen at this very pub two weeks ago: the large and loud Jamie Ballard; Mr. Cowell, the slight farmer from north of town; and, just now entering at the door, the widower Mr. Digweed, whom Miss Whyte considered a friend.

"They do a brisk business," Tinsdale remarked. "Though 'tis early, the Blue Duck's ale still draws 'em."

"Hayden," Perry Wenfield called rudely, interrupting. He rose to his feet and, uninvited, carried his drink over to their table. Placing both palms then upon the worn oak, he leaned across toward Hayden. "The damage you have done—to my father's reputation, to my mama, to me—will be the talk of this county."

"I assure you, Wenfell, 'tis not news I shall carry."

"You need do nothing more! The harm is done!"

"Your father chose his path, sir."

"He is innocent!"

"He was, and is, free to contest any charge. Though I do not believe I made one."

"Because you had no proof!"

"Because I did not need to tender it." Hayden eyed the younger man. "You must ask your father to explain, sir. As I've said, I do not carry tales."

"Oh, you do not, do you?" Wenfield jeered.

Hayden glanced briefly at the busy bar, which had fallen largely silent. Conversation had also stilled among those at the tables and the long settle near the hearth.

"There is a time and a place—" he began.

"Here! Now!" Wenfield started fumbling with his cravat.

"Stay a minute," Tinsdale said, rising. "Let us approach this like gentlemen—"

"Gentlemen!" Wenfield scoffed. *"He"*—and he flung an arm out toward Hayden—"isn't even a *mister!"* He appeared to find this gibe hilarious, and laughed loudly.

Someone must have alerted others of a quarrel in the pub, because the taproom, which just minutes before had seemed peaceful and welcoming on a cold evening, now held an expectant crowd of jostling locals.

Hayden met Wenfield's blazing gaze.

"How much have you imbibed, Winfield?"

"Hardly anything at all! You cannot use a dram of ale as an excuse to worm out of this. And you must know I have told Miss Whyte all that you—"

Hayden rose smoothly to his feet. "You will not bandy names about."

"You will not tell me anything, *Lord* Hayden."

Hayden knew it was truly beneath him to wish to pummel young Wenfield, but he did, and not only for Anne Whyte. He nodded to Tinsdale, who gleefully ordered the tables to be pushed back from the center of the floor. The taproom itself appeared to fill instantly three rows deep with onlookers. Given the pub's low ceiling, and the crowd's gaping mouths, Hayden thought them all likely to run out of air.

"I cannot abide a fella," Hayden told Wenfield very evenly, "who does not comprehend his own good fortune."

"You were handed everything!"

"As were you."

Wenfield paused only briefly. "I haven't as much now, have I?" he countered.

"That is certainly something to question. I would think you unaccountably fortunate. Were *I* as fortunate, I would not be sulking in this pub."

"No? Well, you're likely to be even less fortunate shortly, once you're acquainted with the floor!"

This drew laughs. A brisk business in wagers had begun. Tinsdale was happily accepting them, at thirteen to one in Wenfield's favor. Perry Wenfield's face broke into a confident smile at hearing the odds and the repeated exclamations of "Done!" Hayden gathered that Wenfield must have sparred successfully before. He watched little Po Cowell, the father of eight, now pushed into duty as referee. Cowell shuffled obligingly toward them.

"Gen'lmen," he said. "I understand you wish to mill."

"It seems Mr. Wenford is set upon it, Mr. Cowell."

"I am," Perry affirmed. "And my *name,* you mutton-head, is *Wenfield.*"

"Oh, I knew *that.*" Which comment served, as Hayden knew it would, to infuriate his opponent. Wenfield would have lunged at him right there had Cowell and Ballard not held him back.

"We'll fight fair now," Cowell said, with a firmness belied by his small size. "I'll make the mark with this charcoal." He held up a piece from the hearth. "My boy Eddie here will keep the watch. Two-minute rounds. And a minute between, gen'lmen?"

"Half a minute," Hayden said. Perry Wenfield's eyebrows rose, but he nodded.

"And we'll go—" Cowell began.

"Not long." Wenfield smiled.

"As long as it takes," Hayden said.

"Right then, until one of ye concedes. No hits below the waist. An' no wrestlin'. This be your corner, sir." Cowell indicated almost precisely where Hayden stood. "An', Mr. Wenfield, you be over here." He gestured across the now open floor. "We begin as soon as ye've stripped and set your seconds."

Wenfield had apparently picked Ballard to aid him. Hayden looked to Tinsdale, who was too busy betting to consider fetching a jug of water and a towel. Hayden's gaze sought any familiar face and settled on one of the stable lads from the inn. *If he can look after my bloods,* he thought, *he can look after me.* At Hayden's nod the boy hurried over. Hayden suspected the lad would have performed any task for sheer entertainment, but the promise of half a crown ensured his attentions.

Wenfield was wasting energy in a great rush to rid himself of his clothing, and wasting his breath on laughing and crowing to the onlookers. Hayden calmly tossed off his cravat, shifted—with the boy's help—out of his coat, and shed his waistcoat. Despite the large fire and packed room, he felt chilled in his shirtsleeves, but he knew he would be heated soon enough.

He loosened his cuffs and swiftly drew his shirt over his head.

"A pub, a mill, and *Hayden*," Tinsdale pronounced with relish, turning to him. " 'Tis the complete thing!" As he looked at Hayden, he seemed to collect himself. "I say, is there anything you need?"

"Send someone over to the inn for Phipps. I shall want to fit back into my coat."

"Certainly."

Hayden wished for someone of sense about him. His cousin Chas would have done, or Demarest or Knowles, or even David—in a pinch. As he sat to have the stable lad pull off his boots, he looked at the room as though it were quite apart from him. The crowd awaited a mill; they would watch and wager, perhaps changing their bets round by round. But they would have been equally enthusiastic about a cockfight; they would have exclaimed lustily at a bull-baiting, or any public display that enlivened their days. The local folk, from stable lads to Lord Tinsdale, did not distinguish their amusements.

For a moment, Hayden felt repulsed. He glanced at his hands. He had not fought barefisted in years. He *had* fought, and often, but among his set—at Jackson's or in a private venue. He abhorred the public circus. He had to wonder what he had come to, to find himself in such a leveling circumstance.

His gaze settled on Perry Wenfield. The younger man looked fit, and he was easily a stone heavier than Hayden. But he did not have the height or the reach—and he could not have had the experience, else he would not be expending so much breath now in his agitated rodomontade. No doubt Wenfield considered himself a Corinthian, a sportsman of the first order. But Corinthians were gentlemen of modesty; they did not fight out of temper, nor would they abuse horses, as Wenfield did.

They would not toss Miss Whyte's name about in a pub.

Hayden rose to his feet. He knew he was not fully recovered from his illness. But strength alone had never made for the best performance. If anything, he must master the urge to let fly. He had wanted to pound Perry Wenfield from the first, when the blighter had come calling on Anne Whyte while Hayden lay abed upstairs. That had been unacceptable—that Wenfield should dare call upon the lady Hayden had chosen for his own. And he *had* chosen, he realized, even then. He still chose. Perry Wenfield must better him here, in the Blue Duck pub, to compel him to leave off. And even then . . .

He stepped up to the scratch in his bare feet, stripped to the waist and with cold purpose in his heart. He extended his right hand to shake Wenfield's, but his adversary refused to reciprocate.

"You shan't have her," Wenfield grated. His fists were already clenched.

"Perhaps not. But I shall shut your mouth."

Mr. Cowell's gray eyebrows shot high. He gave the signal, and at once they were circling.

For a few seconds, Hayden still heard the crowd; he was aware of the press of people. He heard Jamie Ballard loudly insisting that Hayden had been the "swooning gent" and offering very long odds. Blustering sorts like Ballard, who understood only the most brutish confrontations, were ill equipped to analyze the more schooled adversaries. Hayden closed his ears and concentrated on gauging Wenfield for himself.

As they assessed each other, both kept their guard up, fists raised above extended forearms. Then Hayden initiated a series of swift jabs to Wenfield's jaw—all intended to measure the strength of that guard. Wenfield was quick, but not quick enough. The last jab connected, throwing his head back and pulling him off balance.

Wenfield came back with a rush. For a moment they traded

blow for blow. Hayden intended each strike to knock Wenfield down. He succeeded twice, to have Wenfield return to his feet dazed. Wenfield was less discriminating with his aim. Clearly, he wanted to punish, to smash and pound, which Hayden had not permitted him to do. When Wenfield's patience broke, and he swung wide with his right, Hayden could not entirely evade the strike. But he took advantage of the opening and closed for a swift right hook to Wenfield's chin.

Wenfield went sprawling. The hum of the crowd temporarily hushed. But Hayden's opponent was soon on his feet and glowering vengefully. Hayden had to admit that Perry Wenfield was game. How long he might prove so was another matter.

He kept to his strategy, which was defensive. Wenfield, perhaps intent on recovering his standing with the crowd, was dancing around, foolishly expending his reserves—and lowering his guard. Hayden managed to strike him twice for each hit taken. By the end of the third round, Wenfield seemed to realize that agreeing to an inadequate half-a-minute rest between rounds now granted him little chance for recovery, and that Hayden, who was still breathing easily, knew it.

"He is catching on," Tinsdale whispered to him during the break. "He will stop the lunging and do as you do."

Hayden shook his head, while letting the stable lad wipe his dripping brow. "No. He will continue as he is."

And in the next round that indeed proved to be the case. Wenfield, eager for a dramatic strike, rushed to connect, only to have the force of his blows deflected by Hayden's steady guard. Hayden persisted in targeting Wenfield's face, with hits that told against his jaw, cheek, neck, and ear. Again, in his eagerness, Wenfield surrendered the balance and strength of his legs to press a marginal and imagined advantage of weight—and once more was sent to the floor.

He returned to charge and catch Hayden in the left side, just below his ribs. The force of the attack knocked the breath from him, but Hayden remained upright and maintained his guard. Wenfield had never yet struck his face—he hadn't the reach or technique—though Wenfield's own features were starting to discolor with blood and bruising. One eye was nearly swollen shut. Both he and Hayden were bathed in sweat, and their bare hands were raw with punishment.

In the fifth round, feeling the exhaustion of constant vigilance, Hayden let his guard down temporarily, and Wenfield caught him with a blow to his left cheek. The crowd cheered. As he briefly stumbled, Hayden felt the blood in his mouth. But he could now read Perry Wenfield's gaze and silently vowed that the man would not catch him again. He heard someone yell odds—which were still long in Wenfield's favor—but Hayden's resolve was steady. Despite recognizing a limit to strength and stamina imposed by his recent illness, the ground was his. He had the speed, the skills, and the *science* to carry this to victory. Wenfield would be the one to give way.

He concentrated on landing another knock-down blow, and with his right soon succeeded in jabbing Wenfield's surprisingly soft belly.

Another cheer arose from the growing crowd as Wenfield fell to his knees. The rabble, Hayden reflected, loved drama even more than the triumph of its hero. But again Wenfield rose and ran wildly at Hayden, who sidestepped the charge.

"Confound it!" Perry panted, furiously raising his fists again, "You ain't human!"

Wenfield should have saved his breath; he was not recouping enough of it between rounds. Indeed, Hayden admitted to fear that in his own case this exercise, so close upon his recovery, would provoke his cough. If need be, he would fight on with Anne Whyte's last lozenge between his teeth—a use, he knew, of which she would scarcely approve.

At thought of Miss Whyte, Hayden advanced with a desire for blood, and rammed home a powerful punch to Wenfield's left side, again sending the dasher to the floor.

In the firelight and lantern light, their bodies shone with exertion. As Wenfield struggled to come up to scratch, a slight figure flew from the corner of Hayden's vision. Anne Whyte placed a deliciously cool palm against his chest. Her right hand stopped Perry Wenfield's arm. She stood between them, over Mr. Cowell's protest and the crowd's curious hush.

"I've told you," Hayden breathed heavily, "not to fling your-self . . . before objects."

"You are not *objects!* You are *men!*" Her gaze was on Hayden's swollen lip. "This is barbaric, senseless!" She glanced at Wen-field, then again into Hayden's eyes. "Can you not use your *minds?*"

Hayden slipped his right arm about her waist—something he had wanted to do ever since seeing her dance—and, lifting her, swung her easily to the side behind him. Cowell had not called "time." As Wenfield's attention shifted from Anne Whyte, Hayden sent a strong, unerring left to her suitor's pretty nose.

The blow snapped Wenfield's head back. He again fell to the floor. As Mr. Cowell rather rudely pushed Anne away, the crowd erupted. The commotion was deafening.

"He's drawn his cork!" Lord Tinsdale enthused. "Now we shall see something!"

Anne turned to him in horror.

"You will not stop this?"

"Stop it? Heavens, no! Miss Whyte, do step aside here. You might be hurt."

Hurt! Anne swallowed as she watched the two men battling before her. She was repelled by the exhibition: by the crowd and its enthusiasm; the warmth and press of bodies; the brutish blood and sweat. Just then she could actually *hear* the thud of a fist against flesh. For a second she closed her eyes.

"Are you here alone, Miss Whyte?" Lord Tinsdale shouted in her ear, even as he continued to take bets.

"No." Anne looked to the side. Ned was nowhere to be seen. "My father's man drove in with me."

"Good thing your father, Mr. Whyte, ain't magistrate yet. Else he'd feel obliged to stop this!" Tinsdale smiled.

Anne glanced at him impatiently before her attention focused on Hayden.

Her first thought on entering the raucous taproom had been to stop the clash. She had taken time only to identify Hayden and Perry Wenfield before impulsively pushing her way to the center of the room. She knew she had to be in some manner responsible for this bout; she had felt it right to intervene. But now she numbly watched the two men fight, and of the two, the one who drew her attention was Hayden.

Looking at his glistening torso, she recalled the feel of his damply muscled chest against her palm. It did not seem possible that this impressively fit gentleman had been flat on his back three weeks before. She watched his arms, fists held out before him in that sturdy defense. Every motion of his was deliberate. The movements even had an elegant economy, like a dance. Of the two men, he seemed still to have strength in check; though both were breathing heavily, only Perry Wenfield appeared to be tiring. Hayden ducked another wide swing from Perry, then moved to strike quickly again at Perry's injured face.

Anne felt ill.

"When will it . . . when will it end?" she asked Tinsdale.

"I cannot say when, Miss Whyte." His gaze never left the combatants. "But I might tell you *how*. Hayden mills 'em down. Believes it's always best to have an opponent yield, so there's no hard feeling! Most of us can't stomach it; takes more stamina this way, you see. There's barely time between rounds here for a man to catch his breath. That's why Hayden holds the record for rounds at Jackson's."

Perry Wenfield appeared to close just then, managing a wide swing to Hayden's ribs.

"And what 'round' is this?"

"Nine. No—"

"Ten, m'lord," the stable boy piped, his voice high with excitement.

"Ten, is it? Good lad." Tinsdale absently patted the boy's shoulder. "Should end soon, though, since Hayden's not quite up to his usual form. All the same, see how quick he pops one there, Miss Whyte! You've none of the home-brewed with Hayden. I tell you, 'tis a pleasure to watch his style. Wenfield's trying to rally, but—there! A swift left, straight to the jaw! Neat, *neat!* Wenfield left himself open for that. What a face he will have!" As Anne turned away, Tinsdale added, "Wenfield has bottom. But you should have chosen Hayden, Miss Whyte."

"I have not chosen anyone, my lord."

"No?" Tinsdale's bright gaze briefly left the fight to find her own. "That's the trouble, then. Ah, Mr. Digweed." Tinsdale laughed. "I believe you called this correctly, sir."

"It does seem likely, my lord." Though he was clearly pleased with the event, Thaddeus Digweed looked keenly at Anne. "Should you like to leave, Miss Anne?" he asked. "I would escort you out."

"You're very kind, Mr. Digweed." She had to shout over the noise. "But I shall stay until the end." *When one or both might need my aid,* she added silently.

"You cannot leave now in any event, Mr. Digweed," Tinsdale protested. "Not when you shall have a fortune."

"Surely you haven't wagered, sir?" Anne asked Digweed, recalling her father's discussion of how deeply indebted the older man was. "To risk so much—"

"Someone must win, lass," he commented. "An' I'm due for a turn of luck."

Anne shook her head, then dared to glance over her shoulder. Perry Wenfield, his shoulders stooped with exhaustion, his face swollen beyond recognition, still essayed an occasional weak punch against Hayden's implacable guard. Hayden's bare fists, still held high before him, were torn and red with blood. Anne recalled how immaculately he had kept his hands, and stared at them now with a sense of her own impotence. His lip was bleeding . . .

With dedicated attention, Mr. Cowell stepped ably about the combatants. Anne sensed that some climax pended, but its nature hardly mattered. She simply wanted the ordeal over.

The two men traded blows to the body, then Perry's heavy arm swung high in another attempt at Hayden's face. But the swing was wild, and Hayden drove in at once with his left, to slam Perry most accurately on his already bleeding nose.

Perry howled and fell to his knees. The onlookers roared. Mr. Cowell leaned to speak to Perry, then turned to Hayden—and raised his left arm.

"Yes. Yes," Mr. Digweed repeated happily, shaking Lord Tinsdale's hand. "I thank you for your tip, milord. Miss Whyte." And he departed eagerly with his winnings.

Lord Tinsdale looked thoughtful. "I did not expect that.

Hayden ended it earlier than I'd have guessed. Lost me some pennies, there! But then, he's not looking quite up to snuff . . ."

Anne pushed her way into the crowd, which was not as exultant as she would have anticipated. Perhaps they had wanted more, or most had bet against Lord Hayden. Indeed, that surely must have been what Jamie Ballard had done; he had been loud in convincing the room that Wenfield would prevail. He leaned over Perry Wenfield now, his face twisted with angry disappointment.

Anne took one last look at Hayden's gleaming back, just as his valet, Phipps, eased a shirt over his head. Then she looked away.

"Mr. Ballard," she said abruptly, "won't you help Mr. Wenfield to a seat?"

Ballard grumbled and did as he was asked. But he did not stay. Anne took a close, horrified look at Perry's face, then turned to Hayden, who still had his back to them.

"You are a beast, my lord," she said clearly. "A brutish, savage beast."

He turned about slowly. His shirt was open at the throat, his coat unbuttoned. His own face was far from undamaged, with that bleeding lip, a cut across one temple, and a blooming bruise upon one cheek.

"There were two of us, Miss Whyte," he said sharply. "I believe Mr. Cowell will confirm the match was fair."

"Fair!" She gestured at Perry's face.

"If you no longer want him so, that is, of course, your choice. But I did not know you objected to patients."

"You have left him a casualty of war!"

Hayden gave her a brief, stiff bow.

"Any soldier would welcome your attentions," he said lightly, though his gaze was as dark as his bruised cheek. Then he, Phipps, Tinsdale, and a good part of the village spilled out of the pub and into the dusk.

Chapter Thirteen

I rushed into town to see him, Vee," Anne admitted, pacing her friend's parlor. "I felt I must follow him, to thank him for something he had done for Father." She paused and looked beseechingly at Vera. "Instead I find the whole town watching him *perform*—with such violence!"

"Young Nate was there in the taproom. Delivering a message to Mrs. Midgeley for me. He says Mr. Wenfield provoked it."

"I do not care who provoked it. It should never have occurred. Between two such gentlemen—one of them a marquis!"

"Men will mill, Anne. Perhaps you condemn them so because of your own part in their dispute." At Anne's questioning look, Vera added, "Both of them seek your favor."

"Mr. Myles—Lord Hayden—does not."

Vera's eyebrows rose. "Do not be obtuse, dear. It is not like you."

Again Anne paced. "He cannot do so. He should not. He is a peer."

"That is not all he is. You tell me he left Wiswood because Perry Wenfield's offer stood, and that you had not answered it."

"I *had* answered it."

"But you did not reveal as much to Lord Hayden. You implied you still considered it. You lied to him, Anne."

Anne's chin rose. 'Lied' is rather strong."

"Is it? It is no stronger than that of which you accuse him, in posing as *Mister* Myles. At least that *is* his name—one of them." Vera looked down at her sewing. "You should press him regarding this business with the Wenfields. I suspect honor keeps him silent—when he fears you plan to become one of the family."

"I had not thought of that."

As Anne worried her hands, Vera asked, "Shall I send Nate for Lord Hayden?"

"I . . . I am not at all certain he would come."

Vera looked askance. "That may be, of course. But I imagine that if the vicar requested his presence, he might welcome the opportunity to explain himself."

"He might have left."

Vera set her work aside and rose to her feet. " 'Tis most unlikely Lord Hayden would have departed in the dark this evening. He has no reason to skulk about. I shall just go ask Clement to pen a note."

Once Vera had gone, Anne took a seat, only to rise straightaway and pace once more. Certainly she *had* given every impression that she entertained Perry Wenfield's suit. Certainly Perry would have given that impression. They had been surprised, after all, in what amounted to an embrace. But Lord Hayden had had no hint of an engagement when he first dissembled. Vera had to be mistaken. Hayden must have had another reason for withholding his name, or he had simply been funning, as Anne understood so many members of the *haut ton* were wont to do. She'd had proof of his eccentricity, of the peculiar nature of his amusements, in the pub that afternoon.

For some minutes she could do no more than stare abstractedly at the fire. She would not soon forget Lord Hayden sparring. His coats certainly slimmed his shoulders . . .

"Nate is off," Vera announced on returning, "and Clement and I will happily share a crumb with Lord Hayden at a late supper, should he arrive with an appetite. But you say he was injured?"

"A little. Not badly. Not as badly as Perry Wenfield, who has a broken nose."

" 'Twill distinguish him in future, Anne." Vera had taken up her needlework once again. "I suggest that you put Mr. Wenfield from your mind, and concentrate on Lord Hayden. You did tell me you came into town to speak with him."

"Yes."

"And so you shall."

Anne glanced at her suspiciously industrious friend. "Why do you look so contented, Vee?"

"Because I am amused, dear. You are usually so capable. And I suspect he is as well."

Anne, wishing only to avoid further unsettling conversation, turned to the hall. "I forgot to bring down some preparations for you. I shall just go upstairs to collect them."

A knock at the front door startled her. Anne backed into the parlor as the Spragues' housekeeper opened the door. When Lord Hayden stepped through to the center hall, Anne was discomfited rather than surprised. She had thought to have more time. She had thought, in some manner, to prepare.

His gaze found hers. She thought he attempted a smile. Perhaps only the swollen corner of his lip conveyed that impression.

"Miss Whyte," he said, bowing. "Mrs. Sprague. The vicar sent for me." He slipped his open greatcoat from his shoulders and handed it to the housekeeper.

"Did he?" Vera rose and moved toward him. "I shall see if he is free." And gesturing Hayden into the parlor, she entered the hall and neatly closed the parlor doors behind her.

Anne could hardly believe that in the abbreviated interval since his bout in the pub, Lord Hayden had managed to bathe and dress as neatly as he had. With his inestimable Mr. Phipps, he clearly had no need of anyone else.

"Miss Whyte," he said at once. "I must apologize for my short temper at the pub. I hope Mr. Wenfield improves?"

"He is in the care of others at the inn. He promises to recover in good time, though at the moment he cannot speak." She paused. "You broke his nose."

"Yes."

"You intended to?"

He shook his head. "I simply knew that I broke it."

"You have broken someone else's nose?"

He appeared, as near as possible, to firm his lips. Anne contained her instant aversion to such viciousness. She indicated a seat.

"The vicar will be a minute," she said, knowing Clement Sprague was likely to be much longer than that. She perched on the sofa, only to find that Hayden still stood. "Lord Hayden," she began. "I have not properly thanked you for collecting those letters—for all you have done for my father."

"No thanks are necessary, Miss Whyte. I indicated as much before. Your father is a most deserving gentleman."

"Nevertheless, I do thank you."

He bowed. "You are most welcome."

For some seconds she could do no more than look at him, at his still-damp fair hair and direct blue gaze. But she sensed his expectation. There was, after all, much to say.

"I will not marry Perry Wenfield."

Her simple statement had his eyebrows shooting high.

"On the merits, or merely because the poor man lost at sport?"

"Sport! 'Twas little better than a brawl!"

He smiled, then shrugged. "You and I cannot be expected to agree on every matter, Miss Whyte."

"Why should we agree on *any* matter, Lord Hayden?"

"Because we are friends?" The intensity of his glance took her breath. Aware of a most irrepressible flutter in her chest, she looked down.

"I was given to believe," he said politely, "that you seriously considered Mr. Wenfield's suit."

"I did *consider* his suit, but I decided against it almost as soon as he first offered."

"And when did he first offer?"

"When? Why, I think the day he came to call at Wiswood. When you were ill."

Again he smiled. "Miss Anne, I believe I might now tell you why I did not correct your understanding—that is, why I did not tell you my full name on that very occasion."

"I should not have thought *your* behavior dependent upon Mr. Wenfield's—*my lord*."

"But I assure you that it has been. Inextricably." He stepped closer. Resting one hand upon the mantelpiece, he placed a booted foot upon the shallow brass fender. Though the pose was relaxed, Anne sensed that he maintained his guard—just as she had seen him do in the pub room.

"Titus Wenfield," he began, "that is, the senior Wenfield,

chose to take enormous risks with his finances. Some years ago, he made an extravagant investment that turned out badly. To cover his losses, he decided to bill the tenants at Hollen Hall and to lay the responsibility for their increasingly outrageous rents upon my father, the Duke of Braughton."

At Anne's silently formed "Oh," Hayden smiled slightly. He looked at his hand upon the mantel. She noticed distractedly that his fingers, those that were not bandaged, were scratched and raw. She was amazed that none appeared broken.

"There was a disparity between the monies collected by Wenfield and those forwarded to my father's agent—in essence, a theft. As you might imagine, Mr. Wenfield never anticipated being caught in this thievery. The tenants' complaints about high payments were meant to be lost amid all the distress of these times, as everyone objects to the current elevated prices and taxes. And though my father has a most diligent agent, the accounts naturally never registered more than came into them. Had it not been for a letter to Braughton—signed, among others, by a Mr. E. Whyte"—Anne drew a quick breath—"Braughton would, perhaps, not have addressed the matter until it was too late to recapture any of the funds." He moved away from the hearthside and began to walk about the room.

"When I fell ill in Italy, I thought at first to return to London or home to Braughton, to Leicestershire. But I recalled that my father had wished me to consider investigating the situation that gave rise to such a letter. I have wondered whether that is why I had such a strong desire to revisit Cumberland, a place to which I'd not returned even once in almost twenty years. My father by no means required a visit. A written inquiry to the agent might have sufficed, but as you might properly deduce, such an inquiry would have revealed little.

"Upon my arrival"—he smiled at her—"I was in no fit shape to examine any estate business, but the visit of the younger Mr. Wenfield to your home certainly jarred my memory. I recognized the name and, as this is not the most populous of counties, determined he must be a close relation to, if not the principal tenant at, Hollen Hall. You will recall that at first I thought the gentleman who'd come calling was the elder Wenfield."

"Yes."

"I did, of course, have other reasons for objecting to the call," Hayden added with a significant pause. But as Anne only tilted her head expectantly, he went on. "I had been on the point of correcting your use of 'Mr. Myles.' But I thought the better of it. The name might have prejudiced any effort to uncover the true situation at Hollen. As 'Mister Myles,' I had critical information volunteered to me. Additionally, had Titus Wenfield been alerted to my presence, as 'Hayden,' you understand, I can only guess how swiftly he might have fled the area. He'd have been wise to have hidden his gains, but he had accumulated much to purchase a property on Windermere."

"Yes. Perry Wenfield mentioned it that day he came to call." Struck with the thought, Anne said, "Perry might not know of his father's role."

Hayden shook his head. "He might not have known then. I believe he *must* know now, though apparently he does not accept. Witness the dispute in the pub this evening."

"He fought for his father's honor?"

"Partly. I certainly fought for Braughton's." Again his pause and his look implied much. "What I have relayed to you of Mr. Wenfield's fraud is a most confidential matter. Only the Wenfields, my father and his agent, and Greeley, the former Hollen steward—who faces prison—know of it. Mr. and Mrs. Wenfield sail for Barbados in two days. The tenants at the Hall might suspect something of the business—there is certain to be conjecture—but I am honor-bound not to speak of it. So I must ask you, Miss Whyte, to keep this even from your father, at least in the near term. I tell *you* only because I would have you forgive me for descending to fisticuffs."

Descending! At once she realized what that encounter in the pub had cost him in pride. She also recognized that at its conclusion she had had much too much to say.

"I shall honor your confidence, my lord." She had not intended to sound so stiffly formal. His small smile struck her as strained.

"But I am not to be forgiven for having posed as 'Mr. Myles'? I know I might have confessed even before Perry Wenfield's visit, but for that brief period, for that one day, you did make it so very sweet for me to be *only* your patient."

With some shock, she knew that he had always been more than a patient.

"I think . . ." She paused. "I think you had your reasons. And I was certainly as much to blame for initially mistaking your standing as you were for continuing the error."

"That is most gracious of you, Miss Whyte. No, please do not get up." He moved quickly to the sofa and took the seat beside her. There was not much room. His proximity shortened her breath.

"Perry Wenfield and I," she said, looking not at him but at the fire, "would seem to have fathers in similar situations. They have gone too far. And both have troubled the Duke of Braughton."

"They are not similar, Miss Whyte. Mr. Wenfield's case is so singular that it can hardly be applied to another. And your father simply spoke his mind, or, more accurately, conveyed it in the service of others. He did nothing illegal or mean-spirited. In fact, he has done considerable good. All of us need to be reminded to listen." As she looked to him, he added, "One might consider his willingness to involve himself evidence of a certain carelessness. But I did not collect his letters because I feared for his freedom. I gathered them because I wished to spare *you* distress, and relieve any obligation *you* might feel. Happily, the recipients of your father's letters have proven most prompt and obliging. Though I admit"—and he restrained a smile—"I seem to be benefiting from a good deal of personal advice and instruction."

"You know some of these men?"

"I know them all." He paused. "The only reason I do not yet have all the letters in hand is that messages take a certain amount of time. And much of this has happened quickly, to be sure. Your father told us, Lord Tinsdale and myself, that in his view, once the message has been conveyed, the paper itself lacks meaning. I confess he is in advance of me—or again, less cautious. I should not like the letters held against Mr. Whyte's good name, in any manner."

"You are too kind."

"I cannot be kind enough—Anne." He reached for her right

hand. His own was bandaged, and where it was not bandaged, it was bruised and scraped. Though she was most conscious of his use of her name, Anne was even more aware of the contrast his injured hands made with how carefully he had kept them.

"Your poor hands," she said, turning her own to cradle his. "If you would permit me, some comfrey salve might ease them—"

"'Tis not doctoring I would ask of you now." Though he spoke softly, his tone was grave. Her gaze rose to his once more. "Can you be in any doubt," he asked, "of my meaning?"

"This is . . . too soon."

He smiled as he shook his head. "It has been a very long time coming. And at that, I knew almost instantly."

"You were ill."

"I am still. I am quite lovesick, Anne." Both his hands clasped hers. He sat so close that she fought to breathe. She could see the depths of color in his eyes.

"But you have . . . another lady," she said softly.

"Do I?" He smiled. "I was not aware of it."

"I saw you. At the inn. After the dance—"

"You saw Miss Elissa Birdwistle, now the Honorable Mrs. Henry Purvis, who required the use of my coach. That is all."

"She kissed you!"

He tugged gently on her hand to draw her closer. "Just so. *I* did not kiss *her*." He bent his head to her ear. "I should very much like to kiss *you*, Anne."

She pulled her hands from his and abruptly rose to her feet. He was necessarily compelled to follow. When he stood so very near, she had to tilt her chin to look straight into his eyes.

"I must ask you your intentions, my lord."

"My intention—and there is only one—is to have you call me 'Myles.'" He reached inside his waistcoat pocket and withdrew a ring, a lovely ring of scrolled gold, with a diamond-encircled sapphire. "'Twas my *grand-mère*'s. She would like you to have it."

"As your—wife?"

Again he smiled. "If you would agree to be so. I would be most humbly grateful." As he made to capture her hand once more, Anne drew back.

"I know you do me a great honor. I do beg your pardon. But no, my lord. I fear I cannot."

He looked stunned.

"Cannot? You *cannot* have committed to another?"

"Of course not!"

"Then why not?"

"You are the Marquis of Hayden. You must look higher."

"There is no one higher. You are stellar, Miss Anne Amelia Whyte."

She dismissed the compliment with a wave of her hand. "You deliberately misunderstand!"

"I do not misunderstand. I deliberately ignore. If you must dwell upon my consequence, you must also credit its presumption. Any difference in station does not sway *me,* thus it should not sway you. And if"—he held up a palm as she would have protested—"*you* are too proud to have me step down, then your father, who is a gentleman, must be made to stand up. He does not seem averse. What the sovereign confers, Mr. Whyte cannot decline. I predict he will be knighted within the year."

"You have planned this!"

"I should hope so. It is my nature." This time he successfully caught her hand. "Would you have me remain alone, Anne? If you will not wed me, than I shan't marry."

"A bold claim, Lord Hayden, and one that I do not believe."

"I am prepared to test it, if that is your wish. Braughton will descend through my brother, David. I imagine *he* might object to your choice, but his future sons might not."

"I would not . . . I would certainly not choose to influence . . . to interfere in such important—"

"You cannot help but interfere, my dearest Anne. I am in love with you." He watched her face. "If I must wait upon your convenience, perhaps I might take a room here with the Spragues. 'Twould be considerably more comfortable than the Blue Duck."

She had to fight her smile. "How am I to consider you seriously, when you jest so?"

"My dear, I jest because you make me desperate. If I must move to Hawkshead for your company, I will do so. Hollen Hall and the Priory are too far, though it would give me good cause to race down here frequently in a curricle, as a former suitor was wont to do." He startled her by moving to kneel rather stiffly on one knee before her. "You will pardon me, I hope. I am sore and ungainly this evening."

As though urged, she lightly placed her hands upon his shoulders. They were as broad and strong as she had noted that afternoon. But his left cheek was lividly purple and that one corner of his lip painfully swollen.

"You do not look much like 'His Resplendence' now."

He laughed. "My man Phipps deserves the credit for that sobriquet, not I." As she disputed that with a shake of her head, he again tendered the ring. "If I were to humble myself more, Anne, I should have very little left to give you."

"It is not . . . not that you must do more. 'Tis rather what I cannot do. And it is insurmountable."

"Surely nothing might be *insurmountable,* when you are at such pains to point out my superior consequence?"

"'Tis *because* of your consequence that the impediment poses . . . such a challenge."

"Dearest, I am intrigued. What can you mean?"

She moved her right hand from his shoulder and placed it against the skirt of her gown.

"You forget that I limp."

"I do forget it. Because it does not signify. You cannot be serious."

"You do not comprehend. You would suffer for it."

When he rose to his feet, he drew her close to him.

"I do comprehend," he said softly, "how *I* would suffer were you to deprive me. If I understand you—for some predicted shame, amid society I would never tolerate—you would deny me a beautiful, kind, and clever wife who happens to limp." He laughed as he at last slid his arms about her waist.

"Perry Wenfield said it was presumptuous of me to think you might consider me, for just that reason."

"Pompous Perry Wenfield is wrong, again, and I am delighted to say that he now *suffers* for it. I think I must go finish him off this instant. I cannot have a man imposin' so upon my affairs." Again he laughed.

" 'Tis no laughing matter."

Instantly he sobered. "No," he agreed. "Because you are clearly, and most surprisingly, afraid. I would not have my Anne afraid of anything."

She focused on his chin. She was very much afraid she could no longer think clearly.

"I am not afraid for myself," she confessed, "but for you."

"Now that is new!" His grasp tightened. "But you would use a limp as an excuse! And a *lame* one at that, for you, more than any, know that I myself have unreliable lungs." His glance was provocative. "Despite our ailments, there is a wide world for us to explore. Will you not grace it?"

"Your responsibilities—"

"Cannot be met without you."

"You *have* been meeting them."

He shook his head. "I have not been alive. I have felt as much. Others have remarked it, to my unending irritation. Only now do I understand their meaning. With your help, sweet, and perhaps some of your potions, I might hope to improve. And with your permission, I shall adore you." His arms were iron. "Do you care for me just a little, dearest Anne? Did you feel nothing for me, before you knew me for a marquis?"

"Of course I . . . You think that I care only for your title?"

"Then you would have had me as 'Mr. Myles'?"

"You did not ask me as 'Mr. Myles.' "

"I ask you now."

As she stared, entranced, into his eyes, he loosened the hold of his right arm about her waist. The ring still encircled the tip of his index finger. He drew her left hand from his shoulder and quickly slipped the ring, warmed by his own finger, onto her hand.

"It looks very well," he said, kissing her palm with satisfaction before firmly repositioning her hand upon his shoulder. He pulled her to him.

The ring sparkled upon her hand. She felt the warmth in his embrace and the insistent beat of his heart. She moved to gently touch his bruised cheek and the fair locks of hair that had always fascinated her.

At her touch he briefly closed his eyes.

"Kiss me now, Anne," he urged, "before the Spragues return. I've no patience to spare."

"The Spragues . . . must have retired some time ago."

"Did they?" he breathed. "How propitious."

Little more than six weeks later, at the New Year's Eve ball at Braughton, a joyful family party, which included the spry dowager duchess, made its way down the dance set. All those present agreed that Lord Hayden and his lady were not only charming to look upon but admirably suited. And indeed, in their love and mutual understanding, the two forever found the utmost felicity.